GREEK MYTHOLOGY

JASON AND THE ARGONAUTS

Stephanides Brothers'

GREEK MYTHOLOGY

JASON AND THE ARGONAUTS

Retold by Menelaos Stephanides
Drawings by Yannis Stephanides

Translation
Bruce Walter

SIGMA

Winner of the Pier Paolo Vergerio European prize
Padua 1989

JASON AND THE ARGONAUTS

Made and printed in Greece
ISBN: 960-425-066-3

20, Mavromihali Street, Tel.3607667, Fax.3638941
GR-106 80 ATHENS

SEAFARERS, heroes or freebooters, pursued by the mighty or in pursuit of wealth; whether they voyaged to distant lands as friends or foes, they always opened new horizons and carved new seaways, and sometimes consciously, at others not knowing what they did, turned the wheel of history onto the course of progress.

TABLE OF CONTENTS

Phrixus and Helle 11
The one-sandalled man 29
The voyage to Colchis 67
The golden fleece..135
The terrible voyage home 163
A dream unrealised..221
The tragic end 229

PHRIXUS AND HELLE

One mild spring day, long, long ago in those distant years when history fades into myth, a lone cloud sailed its stately course across the sky. Upon it sat a beautiful maiden. Her name was Nephele and she was a nymph of the heavens. Travelling on high she could admire the enchanting scene which spread itself beneath her. She gazed down on the wooded mountains and the green meadows, the lakes and the rivers, the islands and the lacy pattern of the coastline, and marvelled at all that beauty which the gods had showered so richly on the corner of the world which they called Greece.

Then, as she soared above the earth, Nephele caught sight of a city far below. Its name was Orchomenus and it was built on a rocky outcrop above the great lake of Copais. A large and beautiful building, no doubt the royal palace, stood proudly at the highest point. Impressed by its grandeur and its marble columns, the lovely nymph flew down lower to examine it more closely. The nearer she drew, the more impressed she became, until finally, unable to restrain her curiosity, she stepped lightly from the cloud and set foot on the great terrace of the palace.

At that very moment, Athamas, the young king of Orchomenus, came through a door onto the same terrace. The moment he set eyes on this fair creature from the skies he stood rooted in surprise – and Nephele, too, gazed at the handsome young man in equal wonder. Then Eros, Aphrodite's winged son, who follows all and sees all, flew invisible towards them and in an instant loosed his arrows at their hearts with unerring aim. So it was that the two young people fell in love and married, and Nephele rose no more into the skies but stayed below in Athamas' marble palace.

The fruit of this union was Phrixus, and his sister Helle, two delightful children whom their happy parents loved above all others in this world. And yet, as time went by, Nephele's happiness began to fade. So long accustomed to the freedom of the boundless air, she could not reconcile herself to the limitations of the life she now led upon the earth. Although she lived in a splendid palace, she felt herself a prisoner. She would often wander out upon the terrace, and as she gazed at the clouds which passed across the sky a great sadness would weigh upon her heart. Times came when she would half make up her mind to leave, but the moment she thought of her children the mood would pass and she would blame herself for allowing such thoughts to steal into her mind. Yet with the passage of the years her sorrow grew so deep that she would lock herself in her chamber and dissolve in bitter tears.

At last a day came when she could endure no longer. She had walked out on the terrace once again, and was gazing with longing at the vast canopy of the heavens when a cloud came down and floated at her feet. This time, Nephele did not hesitate for a moment. Nothing could hold her now – neither her love of children or of husband – and soon, forgetting all she had left behind her on the earth below, she was soaring free once more across the boundless azure of the skies.

Athamas had hardly begun to recover from this blow when an unknown girl appeared at his palace gates. The robes she wore showed that she came from a noble family, but her face was drawn with exhaustion and deep grief.

"My name is Ino," she said. I was a princess of Thebes, the daughter of Cadmus. But the goddess Hera had me banished from that city. She was angry with my sister, Semele, so she punished me for good measure. Since then I have been an outcast, wandering from place to place until fortune brought me to your palace. And now I beg you, if you have any pity, let me stay by your side – even as your slave."

As Ino spoke these words, Athamas said to himself, "How strange! Just as one leaves, so another arrives. Clearly, this is the will of the gods."

"You have come at the right moment," he told her. "Just as you need my help, so I need yours. You shall stay in my palace, and if you wish you may become my wife as well. All I ask is that you promise to love and care for my children, Phrixus and Helle, now that their heartless mother has abandoned them."

"Even if they are not my children," Ino replied, "it is enough that they are the children of my husband. I would be worse than ungrateful if I did not love and care for them like a real mother and a devoted wife."

And so Athamas married the daughter of Cadmus.

In the beginning, Ino truly loved the two children and

cared for them as if they were hers. But when she gave birth to her own first child she began to pay rather less attention to them than before. When she bore a second infant her negligence increased, and when yet a third child came, her indifference hardened into hatred.

Phrixus and Helle led a miserable existence at Ino's hands. They would often go out on the terrace and search the skies in the hope that they might espy their true mother seated upon some cloud, for they always continued to believe that she had not forgotten them. But in vain. Although Nephele never ceased to think of them with love, she stayed well away from the skies above Orchomenus. She could not bear the thought that down there lived her children, who longed to have her with them once again. And even if she decided to return it was now too late, for her place had been taken by another.

A few more years went by. Phrixus had now become a wonderfully handsome young man, and in the fresh bloom of her youth his sister Helle was as fair as a little goddess. And yet, while all the people of Orchomenus looked on them with loving pride, Ino could not even bear to set eyes upon the pair. When Athamas eventually felt the burden of the years grow heavy on his shoulders and decided to proclaim Phrixus his heir and successor, Ino's jealous fury knew no bounds. Without, of course, letting any of her hatred betray itself to her husband, she schemed and plotted night and day to ensure that it would not be Phrixus who succeeded to the throne of Orchomenus, but her own son, Learchus. Finally she decided: the only way to remove the obstacle was for Nephele's son to die. And having made up her mind, she conceived a plan as cunning as it was evil.

When the time to plant the corn drew near, she commanded her most trusted slaves to roast all the grain which had been kept aside for sowing; and when, as was the custom in those days, the villagers came to take the seed-corn from the palace granaries, the grain was all parched and lifeless. Suspecting nothing, the farmers ploughed their fields to a fine tilth and sowed all the rich plain. Gentle rains watered the earth, but time went by and not a single blade of wheat showed its head above the fertile dark red earth, and only a few coarse weeds broke the monotony of the endless bare expanse which stretched around Orchomenus.

"What has gone wrong? Why is the land not clothed in green? What will our children eat? Why are the gods punishing us?" These and many other questions sprang to the lips of the local people. And when starvation began to stalk from house to house, Athamas decided to consult the oracle at Delphi to discover what was to blame and how to turn aside the evil which had befallen them.

This was exactly what Ino had been waiting for. She herself chose the representatives who would be sent to Delphi; and Athamas, who suspected nothing, raised no objection. Ino's scheme proceeded smoothly: having first bribed her chosen people royally, she gave them secret instructions to bring back an answer which she herself had prepared in advance.

And so, when the representatives, who had not needed to go to Delphi at all, "returned" from their mission, they presented themselves at the palace before Athamas and Ino and said:

"Alas, we bring heavy tidings from Delphi. All the gods are angered because Phrixus has been declared heir to the throne of Orchomenus. The earth will never bear fruit again unless the son of Nephele is sacrificed to Zeus on the summit of Mount Laphystium!"

A thunderbolt could not have struck Athamas as hard as the news which he now heard.

"That I shall never permit!" he roared. "I will die myself before I let my son be harmed. And mark my words well: no-one shall learn of this oracle if you value your lives!"

"It shall be as you say," replied Ino smoothly, but she

lost no time in revealing the secret to the women of the palace, and so it was not long before the whole of Orchomenus knew not only of the oracle, but that Athamas intended to defy it.

Phrixus, however, was so popular with the people that no one wished to see him die. A large crowd gathered in the market-place and began an anxious discussion.

"Who can be sure," said many of them, "that after the sacrifice the earth will be fertile once again? What if we have to offer Helle, too, and after that our own children as well?"

"And as if all oracles come true!" added others.

There were also those among them who said, "How can the gods want the blood of an innocent man?"

Just as it seemed that popular opinion would upset Ino's schemes another voice broke in:

"Phrixus is no innocent! The gods are right to seek his punishment!" The cry had been uttered by a woman. Her name was Biadice and she was Phrixus' aunt, having married one of his father's brothers; but what few people knew was the extent of her cunning and malice. At this moment she was seizing the opportunity to be revenged on the unfortunate youth because he had once spurned her lustful advances. And so she now began to tell the crowd how Phrixus had allegedly made a shameless attack on her virtue, and that it was for this reason the gods were angry with him.

This false charge was soon known throughout Orchomenus, and the people's hunger had brought them to such a pitch of desperation that it did not take much to persuade them of its truth and turn them against Phrixus. Until a day before, not a single one of them had wished to see him sacrificed, now they all demanded it as the only way to make the earth bear seed again.

Although Athamas could not bring himself to believe that Phrixus was guilty, the people could endure no more and rose against him. Angry crowds gathered outside the palace, and there were many who were ready to burst in, seize Phrixus and drag him to the place of sacrifice. And while Athamas paced back and forth in an agony of indecision, Ino decided that the time had come for her to add her voice:

"You will have to decide," she said, "and now. Everything Biadice says is the plain truth. If you doubt it, the anger of the gods is all the proof you need. The people have every right to rise against you and demand that Phrixus be led to Laphystium for punishment. Face the facts: the salvation of Orchomenus lies in your hands!"

Athamas saw that he had no other choice. Besides, how was he to know that the oracle was a fake? How could he have imagined that his wife could be so sly, or Biadice such a liar?

And so the sacrifice was decided upon. The son of Athamas was doomed to die for the disaster he had supposedly brought upon the people of Orchomenus.

Phrixus accepted the news of his harsh fate with calm courage. Although he stood accused of a crime he had never committed, he was willing to lay down his life if only he knew that by his death he would save his people from starvation. But on the other hand he was no fool; he saw what lay behind the charge, and that his sacrifice would be in vain. Helle, too, though younger, sensed that a hideous injustice was about to be enacted – but she still had a secret hope.

"Our mother roams the skies," she said to Phrixus. "I am sure she can see everything and will not leave us to our fate."

At sunrise the next day, they took Phrixus and led him up to the place of sacrifice. They did not wish to let Helle accompany her brother, but nothing could keep her away, and she refused to be parted from him. Shattered with grief, their unhappy father followed in their footsteps.

The procession reached the summit of Mount Laphystium and halted before the altar of Zeus. When the soldiers had prepared the pyre for the sacrifice, the priest, a knife concealed beneath his cloak, seized Phrixus by the arm. Hoping for a miracle, Phrixus and Helle searched the sky with anxious eyes. Suddenly they saw a cloud, which drew ever closer. On it, the young people could just make out a tiny dot. Their hearts began to beat in wild hope. Now the figure of a woman could be clearly distinguished. "Our mother is coming!" Helle cried, and, weak though she was, she tried to tear her brother from the priest's grasp. He attempted to push her away, but Helle cried again:

"But our mother is coming! Won't you even let her kiss her children, and bid farewell to a son who's to be slain?" The priest relented. All those on the mountain-top watched the cloud in awe as it rapidly approached. Upon it sat Nephele, returning to her children in the hour of their greatest need. At her side was a ram with a golden fleece that glinted in the bright beams of the sun. All who saw the scene were moved, except Ino, who glared at Nephele with hatred in her eyes. The priest, his heart softened too, relaxed his hold on Phrixus, who ran with Helle into the arms of their mother. Nephele embraced her two children with tears of joy, then, wiping the teardrops from her eyes, whispered urgently to her son:

"Climb on the back of this golden-haired beast. It is a magic ram that can fly through the sky, even though it has no wings. Without any need for you to guide it, it will bear you to distant Colchis, the land ruled by Aeëtes, son of Helius. Seek his protection, and in return make him a gift of the golden fleece, after you have first sacrificed the ram to Zeus. It will prove more precious than he could ever begin to imagine."

Phrixus leapt on the beast's back, while behind him Helle cried:

"Take me, too! How can I stay here all alone?" And she also jumped onto the ram, which immediately rose from the earth before the astonished eyes of the gathered crowd.

"A happy journey to you, my children," called Nephele, as the golden ram with its precious cargo faded rapidly from view. And her words were echoed by their astonished father, who could not conceal his joy at this unhoped-for aid. All who stood on the summit added their farewells, dazzled by the great miracle, and filled with remorse for the fate they had so recently reserved for the innocent young man.

Soon the shining ram was but a tiny golden speck, and then it faded from sight into the vault of the heavens.

...she slid from the slippery back of the golden ram and with a cry of despair hurtled into the void beneath...

Phrixus and Helle flew on calmly and peacefully, filled with boundless joy. They sped swiftly over mountains and plains, then crossed above a broad sea filled with islands of all sizes. How wonderful it would have been if their flight had continued as smoothly as it had begun. But this, alas, was not to be. When they reached the narrow channel which links the Aegean to the Sea of Marmara, the weather suddenly changed for the worse. Heavy black clouds filled the sky, while bolts of lightning and the rumbling of thunder made them fear that the world was about to come to its end. At the same time a furious wind blew up, lashing the air to wild turbulence. For all this, the ram kept straight on course. Helle, meanwhile, was terrified. Her courage failed her as she stared in dread at the stormlashed waves below. Phrixus, calm and brave as ever, tried to reassure his sister, telling her that if she clung on tightly there was nothing to be feared. But Helle, who was not a strong girl, grew more and more terrified, and could not hold her own against the raging storm. Exhaustion and fear had weakened her so much that in the end her grip loosened. By a cruel irony of fate, at the very moment when the first sign of clear blue sky appeared on the horizon, she slid from the slippery back of the golden ram and with a cry of despair hurtled into the void beneath. There was no saving her. Phrixus had lost his sister and now, alone and desolate, he continued his flight with a heart torn by grief. The unlucky girl had died, but her name was destined to remain alive for all time – for the narrow strait in which she fell to her death has been known as the Hellespont ever since. And men say that the flow of the waters through its narrow walls may sometimes rise to a roar and sometimes fall to a murmur, but it will never cease entirely, for its sound is the lullaby which sweetens the eternal sleep of the daughter of Nephele.

At last, the tireless ram brought Phrixus to Colchis, and set him down before the gates of the palace, where Aeëtes himself stood waiting. Impressed by the manner of the young man's arrival, he invited him into the great hall. Phrixus entered with the golden ram, and there he told the king his whole tragic story and how his sister had been lost.

Aeëtes listened to him with grave attention; and seeing the golden fleece of the splendid beast which had brought Phrixus to Colchis, he realised that fortune had smiled upon him. Not only did he receive the young man with an open heart, but he gave him his daughter Chalciope in marriage, and four sons were eventually born of this union.

As his mother had counselled him, Phrixus sacrificed the magnificent ram to Zeus, protector of outcasts, and its skin, which has ever since been known as the golden fleece, he presented to Aeëtes. Delighted with his precious gift, the king hung it from a thousand-year old oak tree in the sacred grove of Ares, and set a fearsome dragon to guard it night and day.

The golden fleece soon proved to be even more precious than it appeared. Unbelievable changes began to take place in Colchis. Poverty was banished from every household, and wealth and abundance flowed across the breadth of the land. Aeëtes himself became the richest of kings, and his army the most powerful in the world. Word soon spread far and wide that all this good fortune was due to the magic powers of the golden fleece. Of course this in turn made the magic ram's hide the target of countless brave adventurers with visions of happiness and wealth for their own homelands and themselves – if they could lay their hands upon it. But one and all lived in fear of the king of Colchis and hesitated to risk their lives in such a reckless venture. And when they learned that the golden fleece was guarded by a dragon which was said to belch flames from its mouth and never sleep, so one by one these would-be heroes abandoned the idea of relieving Aeëtes of his treasured possession.

Yet in the end a man was born who would achieve this impossible exploit – Jason, the hero from Iolcus, finally brought the golden fleece to Greece after interminable adventures and unbelievable feats of daring. But with it he brought neither wealth nor happiness. Perhaps this shows us wealth and happiness are dreams that slip like water through the hands, or again, perhaps the story was intended to hold another message for us. Whatever the case may be, let the reader judge for himself after he has read the whole enthralling story.

THE ONE-SANDALLED MAN

Jason was born in Iolcus, just at the time when the golden-haired ram, bearing Phrixus on its back, was landing in Colchis. And while the birth of a child, especially a male child, is always a source of joy to its parents, the arrival of Jason was a cause not for happiness but for great dismay. Aeson, his father, had long feared lest a boy be born to him – and not without reason. Aeson, son of Cretheus of Iolcus, was the only rightful heir to the throne.

However, when his father died it was not he who became king, but his half-brother Pelias, who had no lawful right to the succession since he was Aeson's brother by another father. But Pelias was a cunning and ruthless man who boasted that his father was the earthshaker Poseidon, and that this gave him stronger claims to the throne of Iolcus than Aeson himself. While Pelias stood in no great fear of his brother, who was a mild and self-effacing man, he was terrified lest Aeson acquire a son. And on this matter his mind was made up. If such a thing were to happen, he would find the means to prevent the boy from growing up and demanding the kingdom which belonged to him. Aeson knew this too, and that is the reason why he was panic-stricken when he saw that his wife had given birth to a son. However, the couple soon decided what course of action they must take. They gave out that the child had been born dead, and having conducted a mock funeral in which they buried a wrapped-up log, Aeson took the baby boy up to Mount Pelion where he gave him to the wise centaur Cheiron to be raised.

Cheiron, who was not merely wise but also a renowned teacher, took pity on the hapless father and willingly accepted the child.

"One thing only I beg of you," said Aeson. "Never reveal whose son this is. I would rather lose my boy for ever than know each day his life were at the mercy of the ruthless Pelias."

But Cheiron was of a different opinion.

"As long as he is still small and weak, your son will be told nothing," he replied, "But when he has grown up and acquired such intelligence, knowledge and strength that he need not fear Pelias, but rather Pelias fear him, then I shall reveal to him whose son he is, and I shall tell him too that the throne of Iolcus is his by right. And this I promise you: I shall do whatever lies within my power to make your son such a man that he will one day be a true hero."

"Wise teacher," Aeson replied, "I know I am not fit to offer you advice. Do whatever you think best, and I shall be grateful to you for ever."

And so Cheiron took young Jason up into his cave to raise him. Philyra, the centaur's mother, cared for little Jason while he was in the cradle, but as soon as the child began to walk, Cheiron himself began to undertake his upbringing.

Under his guidance, Jason acquired a strength and daring second to none. He became a champion with the javelin and the bow, a superb swordsman and a master of the arts of war. Living as he did on Mount Pelion, with its abundant wildlife, Jason grew into a splendid hunter, too – so good, indeed, that he even killed a leopard, a savage beast that had become the terror of the whole region.

With scarcely concealed pride, the centaur watched his pupil drape himself in the great cat's spotted pelt after accomplishing this feat.

"One day," said Cheiron, "this young man will be capable of deeds beyond imagining."

But bodily skills were not all that Jason learnt under the centaur's guidance. Cheiron sharpened his judgement, cultivated his love of learning and instructed him in all the arts and sciences known to man.

For endless hours the wise teacher sat with his pupil and taught him the history of the world. He told him of gods and men, and of all that had come to pass from the most distant times until their own days. Spellbound, the young student heard his mentor tell him of the birth of the world, how Mother Earth had sprung from Chaos, and then of the boundless Heavens, the Mountains and the Rivers, all fair and mighty gods. Next Cheiron explained to him how the plants and animals were formed, and finally how the five generations of men appeared one after the other upon the earth. He told him, too, of how a wondrous world had been created by Love and Labour, and how so much of this had been unnecessarily lost through hatred and evil. Jason listened round-eyed to the tale of the fearsome Battle of the Titans, the greatest war of all times, and learned of the victory of the gods of Olympus and the dominance of Zeus, the god who holds the lightning in his grasp. With a heavy heart he heard of the terrible cataclysm which flooded all the earth and of the harsh fate of Prometheus, who was nailed to a rock in the Caucasus because of his love for mankind. There was nothing that Cheiron did not tell Jason. And so it was that he told him, too, of Phrixus and of Helle, and last of all of the magic power of the golden fleece which was to be found in distant Colchis, hanging from the trunk of a thousand-year-old oak in the grove of Ares.

"And if someone brings this miraculous fleece back here," asked Jason, "does that mean that wealth and abundance will come with it?" Filled with curiosity he awaited his wise teacher's answer.

"That is what everybody says," Cheiron replied, "but it is such a daunting task that no-one can find the courage to undertake it. For Colchis is ruled by Aeëtes, son of Helius, a mighty and powerful king who would stop at nothing to safeguard the golden fleece. And then its safekeeping is in the hands of Aeëtes' daughter Medea, the most powerful sorceress in the world. And yet again it is guarded night and day by a terrible dragon, the offspring of Typhoon and Echidna, which not only never sleeps, but is immortal, too. And last of all, the journey from here to Colchis takes one into unknown seas and wild places and is fraught with a thousand dangers. So who would dare embark on an adventure such as this, whose only certain outcome would be death?"

Jason was deeply impressed by this tale. He lay sleepless for nights on end, journeying in his imagination to distant Colchis, until one day he plucked up his courage and asked Cheiron:

"So is it just an idle fancy to dream of bringing the golden fleece to Greece?"

"No, I at least do not believe so," replied the centaur. "Even the most impossible feats are sometimes within a man's grasp if he has will and strength enough, and a total disregard for death. But then nothing is ever achieved without risk. The world was born out of bold endeavour, and only by more such acts can it move onwards."

"How fair and wisely Cheiron spoke," thought Jason, "and how much nobler, instead of protecting one's own petty interests, to win the whole world's love with glorious deeds!"

Only one sorrow shadowed Jason's happy childhood. Cheiron never told him a single word about his parents.

Whenever he was asked, he would always avoid giving an answer – except for once, when he persisted, and Cheiron had said:

"One day, Jason, you shall learn the answer to your question, and then you will be filled with joy. But a serious reason prevents me from revealing the answer to you yet." And such was Jason's confidence in Cheiron that he controlled his impatience.

When he was twenty years of age, his teacher judged that the long-awaited day had come. Jason was now fit to take on any task, however impossible. And so he took him to one of the peaks of Pelion, from where Iolcus could be seen, and said:

"There is the city where you were born and where your parents live. The time has come for you to find out who you are. I could not tell you until now because you have a deadly enemy, and that man is Pelias, king of Iolcus. Now, however, you have grown into manhood. You are strong enough to face him, and that is why you must learn the whole story. Know then that you are an Aeolian – you come, that is, from the line of Aeolus, son of Hellen, founder of the Greek race. Aeolus had seven sons, of whom Sisyphus was the founder of Corinth, Athamas the founder of Orchomenus, and Cretheus the founder of the city which you see before you. Cretheus' son is your father, and the son of Athamas is Phrixus. In other words, you and Phrixus are related. I tell you this because we have talked much in the past of the children of Athamas and of the golden fleece. Indeed, there is even a prophecy which foretells that just as an Aeolian went on a magic ram to Colchis, so another Aeolian will go once more to that distant land to bring back the golden fleece, the skin of the ram that Phrixus sacrificed to Zeus when he came to earth in the land of Aeëtes. Who that man shall be I do not know. All I do know is that you, too, are an Aeolian, as I have explained to you. However, that is not what matters at this moment. When your grandfather Cretheus died, your father should have become king of Iolcus. Instead, the throne was seized by his brother Pelias, who was the son of Cretheus' wife, but by another husband. To save his life, your father was obliged to recognise Pelias as king and live himself as a common citizen in a poor dwelling on the edge of the city. As for you, however, Pelias, would have killed you if he had learned of your birth. For only thus could he have make sure that you would not cast him from his throne one day. Fortunately, he does not even know of your existence, for your father brought you here for safety as soon as you were born. It is your duty now to overthrow Pelias, since you are the rightful heir to Iolcus, and to rule the city with the wisdom and the love which it has lacked in the cruel years of Pelias' reign. You have intelligence, strength and daring on your side, are capable of great and glorious achievements and will, I believe, make a worthy leader. But I must warn you that it will not be at all easy to dislodge Pelias from the throne. He may not have your strength and youth, but he is cunning and ruthless and will fight you in ways you will not be able to foresee. However, if you show the determination and initiative that I believe you possess, then success will be yours. And now that you have learned all I have to teach you, the time has come for us to part. You know where you must go, who you are, and what you must do. One solemn promise only I demand of you: that however hard you fight, you never stray from the path of honour. Never forget that the wings of virtue raise a man much higher than the wings of evil. And if you should ever forget that, then there is only one thing I can say to you: that I would rather see you defeated than dishonourably victorious. Go now, and may you be a true and upright man to the end. If you wish to thank me, the knowledge that you have stayed true to my teaching will be the greatest satisfaction I could have. There is nothing else I desire."

Moved and pleased by what he had heard, and having

promised never to forget the wise words of his teacher, Jason started off down the mountain. But he had hardly gone two paces when he stepped on the foot of a man who was lying face down behind the cover of a bush. The fellow sprang to his feet, but instead of protesting about being trodden on, he began to stammer nervously:

"I didn't hear anything! I won't tell a word to anyone!" and having repeated this several times, he suddenly took to his heels and disappeared.

"I know just where you're going!" Cheiron shouted after him as soon as he saw him take off in that fashion. "Oh, yes," he added turning to Jason, "I know him all right, a well-known informer, Thersandrus by name. He's running off now to turn what he has overheard into gold. Don't let it worry you, though; he won't get very far. I know what I'm saying."

So Jason forgot about the incident, and turning over in his mind all kinds of wonderful plans for the future he set off quickly down the slopes of Pelion towards Iolcus.

He had come to a rushing torrent, and was about to cross it, when he heard a voice behind him:

"Help me, young man! Please help a poor old woman!"

Jason turned his head, but when he saw who it was had spoken to him, he started in surprise. The old woman must

... You have intelligence, strength and daring on your side,
are capable of great and glorious achievements...

have been a hundred years old, filthy and swathed in rags. Her wrinkled face was a mass of open sores where flies were feeding. Yet Jason did not feel disgust for her, only pity. "Tell me, grandmother, what can I do for you?" he asked, going up to her and brushing the flies away from her face with his hand.

"Thank you for your kindness, my child," the old woman replied. "Most people won't even come near me. I must get over the river, but it's too much for my poor old legs – and of all the people who have passed this way so far, not one has been willing to help me. Ah, why is there so little pity in this world? It's a terrible thing to be old, young fellow – and a hundred times worse when you have no-one to support you."

"Don't grieve, grandmother," Jason replied. "We'll soon have you over." And lifting her up in his burly arms he carried her into the water.

Jason had to walk very carefully, because the current was strong. As it was, rushing waters carried away one of his sandals, and by the time he reached the other side it was nowhere to be seen. He carefully put the old woman down on the other bank and asked if there was anything else he could do for her.

"Farewell, young man," was all she said, "and my

blessings on you." Jason had not gone more than a few steps on his way when he heard behind him a clear female voice crying loudly:

"Jason!"

"Strange," said Jason to himself, not so much because the voice bore no resemblance to that of the old woman, but because it was calling out his name. But his wonder turned to utter astonishment when he turned his head and saw, exactly where he had left the old crone, a tall and lovely woman standing in her place, clothed in royal robes and with a golden wreath bound in her hair. Now Jason understood. It was Hera herself who was calling him by his name. He gazed at the goddess in speechless awe and admiration.

"Jason," she said, "go on your way and I shall always be at your side. I am the old woman whom you helped. Before you came, another passed this way. It was Thersandrus, the man who was eavesdropping while Cheiron was speaking to you. I asked him to help me, too, but he wouldn't even come near me. 'What will you give me, old hag?' he shouted. 'My blessings my son,' I answered him. 'Alas, I have nothing else to give.' 'Then keep them for yourself,' he answered, and burst out laughing, delighted with his own wit. 'Then I give you my curse!' I cried. What more is there to say? He never made it to the other side. His foot slipped on a boulder in midstream and the rushing waters carried him away. And that is why I say: press on boldly, and I shall protect you."

Still hardly able to believe what he had heard and seen, the son of Aeson knelt in reverence before the mighty goddess and then, filled with a new joy and confidence, set off once more upon his way to Iolcus.

As Jason was approaching the city, Pelias came driving out of the great gates of the palace, standing upright in his chariot. But at this moment he had not taken to the streets for a mere pleasure jaunt; he had something else on his mind. He appeared uneasy, and looked at the passers-by one by one, as if he were searching for someone. Yet strangest of all, it was not their faces he was peering at so closely, but only their feet.

Only minutes before, Pelias had received a prophecy from the oracle at Delphi. He had always lived with the fear that someone might take his throne from him, just as he had snatched the reins of power from his brother Aeson. This is why he had sent to the oracle, to learn how he might best deal with such a threat; and the answer he had received was as follows: "beware of the one-sandalled man." Here was the reason why he was now combing the streets and looking down at everybody's feet.

In the meantime, Jason had already entered the city of Iolcus. The people in the streets turned their heads to stare at him, not so much because he was walking with only one foot shod, but because he was clothed in the skin of a leopard, a form of dress which told them much and aroused their admiration.

Jason's greatest wish when he entered the city was to meet his parents, and so he asked where Aeson's house was to be found.

"Who are you, stranger, asking after Aeson?" the townspeople demanded.

"I am no stranger," was Jason's reply. "I too am from Iolcus, but I have been away almost since the day that I was born. Now I am returning to my home, and my first wish is to see the parents I have never known."

While the people were trying to make out who this man could be, and what it was he wanted, a clattering of hooves was heard, and the noise of chariot wheels. A splendid carriage drew near. It was the royal chariot, with Pelias standing tall between the shafts. Immediately the crowd drew aside, leaving Jason standing alone in the middle of the road, where he drew the king's attention like a magnet – for one of his feet was bare. Pelias pulled on his reins in alarm and drew up his chariot before the 'one-sandalled' man. He looked the stranger over from top to toe. Here, indeed, was a man to be feared: young, handsome, strongly-built, and with eyes that mirrored his courage and determination. The leopard skin he wore struck even deeper terror into Pelias' heart – for the man who could vanquish so savage and fearsome a beast as this was clearly no common mortal.

However, once Pelias had recovered from his initial shock he began to think more coolly. "I shall sound him out first," he said to himself. "Nothing is certain yet. I must determine whether he is the man the oracle spoke of, but at the same time show him my power."

"Speak out!" he commanded. "Before you stands Pelias, king of Iolcus. Tell me who you are, where you have come from, and for what reason; and be warned: unless you tell me the truth, you are doomed."

"I am not used to being spoken to like this," retorted Jason, "but I will give you an answer all the same. My name is Jason, and I have come from Pelion. There, the centaur Cheiron taught me two things above all else: to love the truth and never be afraid. But what concerns you more nearly is this: I am the son of Aeson, and you know all too well that the man who stands before you is the rightful heir to the throne of Iolcus. My father concealed

... he drew the king's attention like a magnet – for one of his feet was bare...

my birth from you and carried me to Pelion because he feared for my life. Now the time has come for me to return and demand my birthright – and for you the time has come to make a decision, but one that must be reasonable and fair. After all, we are relations and must resolve our differences in a friendly way. Be that as it may; all I need to know for now is where to find my father's house, so I may run to greet my parents."

When Pelias had heard all this, he no longer had the slightest doubt. Before him stood the man he had been warned to dread.

"There is danger here, great danger," he said to himself, "but everything can be arranged. He is young and impulsive, without a trace of cunning in him, and he is sure to fall into the trap that I shall lay for him." And having come to this conclusion, Pelias put on a falsely welcoming air and said:

"Young man, I am delighted to make the acquaintance of the son of Aeson, you may rest assured of that. I am not as wicked as you may imagine and I would have no objection to passing on the throne to you. All I would need was to satisfy myself that you were worthy to undertake so grave a responsibility, although at first sight there seems little doubt of that. But go to visit your parents now, then come back to see me whenever you like, so that we may talk this matter over as relatives and friends."

Having said this, he gave orders for Jason to be led to his father, swung his chariot round and drove back. For all his assurances however, he thought of nothing all the way home but how to ensure that when the young man came to the palace he would not get out of it alive.

Jason's parents greeted their long-lost son with tears of joy. Relatives and friends came flocking to the house of Aeson, and the table was quickly spread to celebrate the happy reunion. Five days and five nights the joyful feast went on, and each day more family and friends arrived, even from the most distant corners of Greece. Moreover, many of these had not just come to celebrate with Aeson the happy news of his son's return; the majority were there to lend their support to Jason now that he had to face an enemy as crafty and deceitful as Pelias. And when the great feast at last came to an end, they all sat down to find a way of returning the throne of Iolcus to the man to whom it rightfully belonged.

"Pelias told me that he wants the two of us to settle our differences in a friendly way," said Jason, "but I suspect that when I go to see him he will put obstacles in my path and lay down unacceptable terms."

"Listen, Jason," said an old man, "we know Pelias well.

Don't go to the palace alone, or, before you have time to utter a word, one gesture from him will suffice for the soldiers he has hidden behind the doors to fall on you with bared swords."

All those present shared the old man's wise opinion, and so, the next day, when Jason went to the palace it was in the company of his new friends, all heroes whose names were renowned throughout Greece. When this bold band appeared before Pelias, with Jason at their head, the king bit his lip in chagrin and said to himself, "There goes my plan!"

Now what could he do? It was no easy matter to resolve. He sat there for some moments, glaring at Jason and his companions, then in the end he decided to tell the truth.

"I see you have not come alone," he said. "And perhaps that was wise of you. When I spoke to you the first time, I was not entirely frank, but now I shall be. Know this, then: I have received a message from the oracle which warns: 'beware the one-sandalled man.' As you will remember, when I first saw you, you were wearing only one sandal, and you must be well aware that you are he the oracle gave warning of. Besides, you yourself told me clearly that you had come to take my throne. Now, you seem a reasonable man, and I would like you to speak to me as sensibly and frankly as I am speaking to you at this moment. Tell me, what would you do if you found yourself in my position? Would you give up a kingdom you had ruled for twenty whole years, as I have, as easily as that?"

In a flash, the story of Phrixus sprang into Jason's mind. He remembered what Cheiron had once told him, and his thoughts at once took wing to distant Colchis. In his eagerness to perform great deeds of valour, he did not hesitate for a moment.

"If I were in your place," he said, "I would give up my throne only if my rival could prove himself a worthier man than me. And for that reason I would challenge him to perform the most impossible task of all; I would send him to bring back the golden fleece and raise it on Mount Laphystium, above Orchomenus."

Pelias' face lit up with joy.

"Agreed!" he shouted. "And you are all witnesses. I promise to give up the throne of Iolcus to Jason if he can carry out the feat he has himself proposed."

Naturally, Pelias did not declare all this because he had any desire for the golden fleece, but because he was sure that, at some stage in this hopelessly difficult undertaking, Jason would disappear for ever.

But Jason was not alone. The bravest of his friends and relatives were prepared to risk their lives along with him.

That very day they all sat down together to plan this bold and daring mission which was, of course, far beyond the powers of any one man alone. "We are all with You," his friends told him, "and not just we. There are others like us, many others, who will willingly follow when they learn that our great venture is to bring back the golden fleece which bestows wealth and happiness on mankind."

Soon Jason's friends began to comb all the towns and villages of Greece. First blowing a horn to gather all the people around them, they would shout with all their might:

"If you are bold and love adventures into the unknown, if you wish to know foreign peoples and strange lands, if you hope to win glory in helping your fellow men, then come with us to distant Colchis, the land ruled by Aeëtes, son of Helius. A sacred duty calls us there: to carry back with us to Greece the golden fleece, the skin of the wondrous ram which bore Phrixus through the skies to the land of Aeëtes, thus saving him from certain death. This fleece works miracles. It showers wealth and happiness on men. To banish poverty and misery from our land we are ready to scorn all danger and set out for far-away Colchis. Our leader is Jason, the worthy pupil of the wise centaur Cheiron. Hera herself has promised him her aid. You who fear no danger, come with us. Join us in the greatest and most

... Join us in the greatest and most wonderful adventure
the world has ever known...

wonderful adventure the world has ever known: the quest for the golden fleece!"

And having said all this, they would move on to another place and start again from the beginning: "You who are bold and love adventures into the unknown...." Shouting out their message again and again, the friends of Jason combed the whole of Greece, seeking out the bold and fearless.

In the end, fifty heroes gathered in Iolcus to take part in the great attempt. First of all came Heracles. He answered the call to distant Colchis during the most tragic period of his whole life: in a fit of madness brought on by the goddess Hera he had killed all his children, thinking they were dragons. It was a grievous blow to the hero. When he recovered, he could not believe the evidence of his own eyes, and nothing could bring him to forgive himself, blameless though he had been. In his despair, he begged death itself to bring him relief. And so, when he heard that Jason needed help, he did not hesitate for a moment but hastened to Iolcus, ready to risk his life in this splendid cause. With him came Hylas, a young man who had stayed faithfully at Heracles' side through all his troubles.

Others came to Iolcus, too: men such as Theseus, the great hero of Athens; the two Dioscuri, Castor and

Polydeuces, twin sons of mighty Zeus; and Telamon, the bold warrior who was first to enter Troy. Then came Meleager, whom no weapon or disease could harm; then Idas, who like a second Heracles had dared to wrestle with Apollo; and Peleus, who had not hesitated to take on the goddess Thetis, invincible though she was. Admetus, too, arrived, the prince who had yoked a lion and a wild boar to a single chariot. Others came, as well, heroes with very special skills like Lynceus, who had keener eyes than the gods themselves, and Tiphys the helmsman, whose skills no man could match. Then came Echion, a herald and public speaker of such skill that he could persuade the most sceptical of audiences. Then there were Zetes and Calais, the two sons of Boreas, who, having wings like their father, could fly through the sky. And together with these, and many others, came Orpheus, the greatest singer in the world.

Meanwhile, Jason had to find the ship that would carry them to Colchis, and this was no easy matter. No voyage of such length had ever been undertaken before, especially through the dangers of unknown seas. The ship they needed would have to be both large and strong and capable of riding out the fiercest storms. Fortunately, there was a man ready to oversee its building – Argus, the greatest shipwright of his day. When Pelias learned of this, he was none too pleased. Secretly summoning Argus to the palace, he told him:

"My father Poseidon came to me in my sleep and commanded me to tell you to make sparing use of nails when you construct this vessel. If you fear Poseidon, you must do his bidding."

"I fear all the gods, and I will obey," replied Argus; but he realised that the ruthless Pelias had been lying to him and determined that this ship would be built with twice the nails that were usually required, and with all the skill at his command, so that if need be it could withstand a hurricane.

Work began on the ship in a little harbour just outside Iolcus. Plans in hand, the master shipwright roamed the yard unceasingly. The finest craftsmen in the trade were working under his orders. They all laboured tirelessly, and each man gave of his best. A builder such as Argus was almost impossible to please, but in the end every one of them managed to do so. In those days, when men worked in a spirit of friendly competition and a word of warm praise was the highest reward that could be asked for, it was no small matter to receive the congratulations of a master-craftsman such as Argus. And so the work went ahead fast and well. Each piece of wood was carved and planed to its correct proportions with perfect accuracy, then slotted

... The finest craftsmen in the trade were working under Argus' orders...

tightly into place so that no water could come through. Each detail of the work was of vital importance, not only the hull, but the hold, the deck and mast as well. Everything had to be perfect: the oars strong and broad, the openings for them correctly positioned, the rowing benches placed so that they would not tire the oarsmen, and the sail strong and of the proper size. Every single detail had to be faultless – and faultless it was. All that remained now was to smear the whole ship with pitch and then to paint it. When these final tasks had been completed, the fairest, largest, fastest and strongest ship the world had ever known was ready. The work of the great shipwright Argus and his chosen craftsmen, it was built to cut through the water like a dolphin and lead its crew to distant, unknown lands, but able, too, to face the foaming waves and struggle bravely against the wrath of Poseidon.

Jason and his comrades came down to the harbour to admire the splendid vessel. Argus and his skilled helpers looked on proudly, too, as the great ship lay gleaming in the sun. All was now ready; not a single detail was missing. The great sail was rolled beneath the cross-tree, the double tiller was in place at the stern, and at the bow stood the most precious object that the ship possessed: a figurehead in the shape of the goddess Hera, protector of heroes.

Dressed in gold, the goddess seemed to be pointing out the way and ensuring the success of this bold venture. But what gave the figurehead its greatest value was the wood from which the goddess' head had been carved. No ordinary timber had been used; this was a piece from the sacred tree of Zeus, the oak of Dodoni which could prophesy the future to mortals. And this particular piece of the tree had a wonderful power all of its own – it could actually speak. Thus, in times of danger, Hera would be able to advise the heroes what action they should take.

"The help the gods can give to men is beyond all reckoning," said Argus, "if once they have decided to give it. Hera's support you know of, but you have Athena on your side as well. Every night the goddess of wisdom would come to me in my sleep and advise me what I should do to make your ship even stronger and more safe. For while Athena always gives her aid to craftsmen, she also watches over the bold and fearless. You have made the golden fleece your goal. It is a fair and high ambition, and worthy of every risk. You are strong and bold, the gods are with you and men admire your courage. You have a ship the like of which the world has never seen. Set forth boldly, then, and my craftsmen's toil and mine will receive its true reward when you return successful."

"Your good words give us faith and courage, master shipwright," said Jason in reply. "We had hoped for success from the first, but now we are certain of it. But I have one thing more to add: now that the ship is ready, we must give it a name. And I think that there is only one name fitting."

"Argo!" shouted someone.

"Argo!" came another voice.

"Argo!" they all shouted together.

"And we shall all be Argonauts," added Jason, taking Argus in his arms and giving him a hug.

Moved by this unanimous tribute to his craftsmanship, the great shipwright said:

"Now all that remains is to launch the Argo into the sea," and picking up a hammer he told the builders to follow his example and each take up position by one of the supports that held the vessel upright.

"You hold her steady by her sides," he told the Argonauts, and when he had made sure each man was in his place, he lifted high the arm which held the hammer and shouted:

"Ready!" Then, after a short pause, he shouted once again:

"Now!"

On the word 'now' all the hammers came down as one

on the wedges which held the supports in place. The wedges flew out, the supports all fell to the ground, and the Argo was free.

"For the golden fleece!" shouted Jason, while the ship which was to carry them to Colchis slid down the rounded beams beneath her keel and slowly entered the sea.

The heroes immediately moored the Argo with thick hawsers, and there she sat, bobbing proudly on the blue waters, waiting for the bold crew who would sail her on her great adventure.

Now there was no time to be lost. The heroes gathered at the home of Aeson and decided to set sail at dawn. Jason was the last to speak:

"When I promised Pelias to bring back the golden fleece," he said, "I knew how many and what terrible dangers we should have to face. Brave and worthy comrades would be needed for the task. You who have offered your services are all this and more. First Argus offered to build the ship which makes our mission not only possible, but likely to succeed. Then you came forward, Heracles first in rank, heroes all, from every corner of Greece. Tomorrow our daunting task begins. We have a long and dangerous voyage to make, for we must travel until the very ends of the earth, and how we shall reach there none of us knows. Our task is to win the golden fleece, but how we shall achieve that, none of us knows either. And last of all we face the journey back, and an enemy who may hunt us down, and there again we cannot tell what may befall us, or how we shall escape. Yet the presence here of so many brave friends, all determined to risk their lives in our cause, is a promise of success. However, this success will not come unless we work together as one mind and one body. For this we need a leader wise yet bold enough to command the whole expedition from beginning to end. I do not need to say that every one of us here possesses these qualities, but I do believe that there is one among us who surpasses all in intelligence, daring and strength – and that man is Heracles. It is he whom I therefore propose as our leader and call on you all to obey."

But the great hero refused.

"Jason has been our leader from the start," he said, "and so it must remain. I do not believe for a moment that I am better than he. Besides, the idea was his, it was he who gave the promise to Pelias, it is he whom we came to help, and it is he whom we should obey. We are a group of comrades bound not by mere self-interest, but by something stronger; far, far stronger: true friendship and a worthy cause, the two foundation stones of every noble venture.

Let us go forward with Jason as our leader, our goal the golden fleece – and wealth and happiness for our children and all who shall come after them."

With Heracles' words, the question of leadership was settled.

"Let us carry the stores on board now, while there is still light," Jason proposed. "We can sleep on the sand next to the Argo and set sail with the first light of dawn."

Then they loaded all the provisions which had been collected at the house of Jason's father and set off for the shore.

Early in the morning, before the sun had even begun to rise, they were woken by the murmur of voices. At a short distance from the heroes a crowd had gathered to see them one last time and bid them farewell as they sailed away in search of the golden fleece.

The Argonauts rose and made themselves ready. Dawn was beginning to flush the sky when one by one they went on board the ship. All the onlookers gazed at them in admiration. So many famous heroes had never been gathered in one crew before. The crowd approached them, and as each adventurer made his way up the gangplank, a ceaseless buzz of whispers could be heard:

"That's Theseus, the man who killed the Minotaur!"

"Ye gods! Heracles!" murmured another in admiration.

"There's Idas, who fought Apollo for the fair Marpessa!"

"Look, there's Castor, the greatest horse-tamer in the world!"

"And his brother Polydeuces, the champion boxer!"

"And Peleus, son of Aeacus, the finest wrestler of them all!"

"But what's this I see? Here are two with wings!"

"Those are the sons of Boreas, the mighty god who brings the cold north wind!"

"And there is Lynceus, the man whose eyes can pierce the darkest night and thickest fog. Why, they say he can even see through clouds and mountains!"

"There's Melampus, the famous physician and seer!"

"And Mopsus, another great soothsayer!"

"And Meleager!"

"And Augeias, son of Helius!"

"And Telamon!"

"Here comes Echion, the smooth-tongued man who can vanquish his enemies with words!"

"And Laertes from Ithaca!"

"There go Peirithous and Polyphemus!"

"And Tiphys and Euphemus!"

"And that one with the lyre. Who is it? Can it be Orpheus?"

"Yes, it is he, the finest singer the world has ever known. His weapon is his lyre. With it he defeated Charon himself!"

Finally only Jason was left on shore. They all wanted to shake his hand, but made way to let the hero's parents through. Aeson clasped his son tightly in his wrinkled arms. Weeping, his mother kissed her son, and on her cheek his own tears mingled with hers.

Only one figure was missing from the send-off. This was Pelias, who stayed behind in his palace, livid with rage to see how many heroes had hastened to Jason's aid.

"But so much the better," he decided in the end. "They all hate me, so let them sail off to their doom if that's what they want."

Jason was just about to go on board when Acastus, the son of Pelias, came running up. Seeing so many brave fellows setting off for Colchis, he wanted to join the expedition, too. But he had reached his decision only at the last moment, on learning that Argus had ignored his father and used plenty of nails in the ship's construction.

"I'll risk my chances along with you," he said on seeing Jason. "My father must be made to understand how unjustly he has acted."

Jason threw wide his arms and embraced the young man,

and still arm in arm they went on board the Argo, to the wild cheers of the crowd.

The time had come to cast off. An offering was made to the gods. It was Jason himself who performed the ceremony, pouring sweet red wine into the sea.

"For Colchis! For the golden fleece!" they all cried.

The heroes sat down at the oars. Tiphys the helmsman went to the sternpost while keen-eyed Lynceus took up his station at the prow.

Jason ordered the mooring ropes to be untied.

"A fair voyage and a safe return!" the onlookers all shouted.

" – and with the golden fleece!" others added.

The oars dipped, the water was churned to foam, and the great adventure into the unknown began.

Once the Argonauts had rowed the Argo from the shelter of the shore, they let down her great, wide sail. It immediately bellied in the wind and gave the vessel new swiftness. The mariners shipped their oars and went back up on deck. Moved by the gallant sight, the crowd on shore waved hands and headscarves in a final farewell to the daring venturers.

The sun rose blood-red from the sea. Orpheus' fingers

struck the chords of his lyre with force, and then his echoing voice sprang from his swelling lungs.

A shudder of delight ran through the Argonauts as they listened to Orpheus' song. No ears had heard a voice like this before, no fingers coaxed such music from a lyre. One by one, the heroes chimed in, captivated. Orpheus' majestic voice rang out above them all, while they joined in with spirit, filling the sea around them with wild notes and stirring verses which carried to the shore like a brave forecast of the triumph which was to come.

Orpheus, matchless singer and poet, gave wings to these heroes who were plunging in where duty led:

We go to an unknown land
By unknown ways.
The immortal gods know our fate
But we can only dare and trust.
Our hearts are afire!
Their flames fed by our glorious dreams.
We are setting off to bring the golden fleece!
We are sailing to bring beauty back to Greece!

The watchers on the shore stood silent. Such moments came but once in a thousand years. With tear-brimmed eyes, Aeson and his wife lived through the most wonderful minutes of their whole existence, a time of parting though it was.

The ship drew rapidly away. The song of the Argonauts faded, and the sun slowly rose before the Argo as she sailed into the East.

Soon the singing could be heard no more. The bold adventurers were now far away on the horizon, while above them the sun shone in all the glory of full day. Finally the Argo was nothing but a tiny speck, slowly disappearing in the waves. Yet Aeson could not tear his eyes from the sea. "Who knows if I shall ever see my son again," he said. "Who knows what lies in wait for them upon their way, or whether they will succeed in bringing the golden fleece back to Greece? Whatever the outcome, a sacred aim like this is worth the risk. I shall steel my heart and wait." Seeing the salt tears on his wife's pale cheek, he wiped them tenderly away and added, "That is what we both must do." And taking her by the arm he led her slowly back to their humble dwelling.

THE VOYAGE TO COLCHIS

Once they were on the open sea, the Argonauts steered due east. Where exactly Colchis lay they did not know, but Cheiron had once said that it was to be found beyond the three seas, far away to the sunrise, where the titan Prometheus hung nailed to a rock above the foaming waves.

So many terrible things were rumoured about these distant seas that had any man believed them all he would never have dared make the voyage. But the Argonauts scorned all danger. Confident that they would overcome every difficulty, and comforted by the hope that the gods would help them, they pressed boldly on.

After a long and tiring sail they reached the island of Lemnos, where they decided to make their first landfall. They needed to rest a little and take on water and supplies to be able to bend to the oars once more with renewed strength. However, on this island so great a temptation lay in wait for them that the expedition to Colchis almost stopped right there.

At that time, only women lived on Lemnos. The menfolk of the island had treated them so cruelly that, unable to bear the tyranny and humiliation any longer, they had secretly armed themselves, set upon the men, and after a murderous struggle chased them from the island. The men of Lemnos had gone, but many others now saw this as a perfect opportunity to rob and loot. So warlike were the island women, however, that all who rashly set out on such raids regretted it bitterly. All they managed to do was to fire the Lemnian women's determination never again to allow males on their island.

So now, when they saw a ship come in, and carrying so many men on board, they immediately took up arms and with their queen, Hypsipyle, at their head went down to the shore, ready to give battle.

When Jason saw the women waiting for them, armed to the teeth, he called for Echion and said, "These women are intent on war, and only you can persuade them to lay their weapons down. We have not come here for a fight, especially one with women. Explain to them where we are headed for, and make them understand, as only you can, that we want nothing but a little water, food and rest."

Jason had chosen his spokesman wisely, for Echion had been taught the art of rhetoric by his crafty father Hermes. His manner was so lively and convincing that he could make his listeners believe the most incredible tales.

The great speaker stepped forward to the bows, but he had hardly opened his mouth when he was greeted by a chorus of jeers and catcalls from the women. With a friendly smile on his face that made him look as handsome as a god, he waited patiently until their threats and curses had died down, and then began to speak.

"Listen to me..."

But again the women shouted him down, brandishing their weapons menacingly.

Echion simply waited with the same patience as before. This was repeated five or six times until the women either grew tired or curious to hear what this patient stranger had to say, and let him utter a few words. Then Echion said:

"If you only knew what it is we want, and why, I am certain you would treat us with more kindness. Let me speak, I beg you."

This appeal to their good nature robbed the women of their words. Vexed, they all turned to Hypsipyle for guidance. Then she shouted to him:

"Say what you have to say, and on your way! Don't waste your time persuading us to let you come ashore."

But this lead was all that Echion required. He began to speak, unhurriedly, but in such persuasive tones that he had no difficulty in breaking down the women's resistance and soon had them hanging from his lips in breathless silence. He told them who they were, where headed for and what their goal. Then he conjured up imaginary lands, insuperable obstacles, and their unbending will to overcome them all and face every danger, even death, with a smile upon their lips.

"We wish you no harm," he added in conclusion. "Had that been the case, we would have charged ashore by now."

But the women had softened towards him already. Their anger had died out entirely, to be replaced by admiration.

"He looks like Apollo!" murmured one of them.

"And he speaks like Hermes!" said another.

..."We wish you no harm. Had that been the case, we would have charged ashore by now."...

"As if honey dripped from his lips!" added a third.

"And they all look like gods, true heroes!" said many others.

Having told them with disarming frankness exactly what it was they wanted, Echion added one final word:

"If you still do not wish to receive us, and look on us with fear, it does not matter, we shall leave. We understand your hesitation, and feel no ill-will towards you. There are other islands near at hand where we shall find a welcome."

Echion's closing remark melted the women completely and finally persuaded even the most sceptical of them that the only decent course was to extend these strangers their hospitality.

However, there was one among them whom Echion's fine words had not impressed one whit, and for a very simple reason: she was stone-deaf.

"What are you about to do?" she shrieked. "I am certain that these fellows are all pirates from Thrace who have found their way here with our husbands' help. Let them set foot on the island and we are doomed!"

"Pay no attention to her!" shouted Polyxo, Hypsipyle's wise old nurse. "We must invite these men into our city and offer them the welcome they deserve."

Hypsipyle, however, knew that her responsibilities as

queen were grave, and was in no hurry to succumb to Echion's charms. Drawing her women aside, she said:

"We have heard fair words from the ship, but I do not think we should place too much trust in them. Words often deceive. So I suggest that some of you run to fetch our best wine and ample quantities of food and water. We shall make a gift of these to the strangers and then beg them to be on their way. That is our wisest course of action, for else a day may come when we say 'if only we had all been deaf!' We must not lėt them come into our city."

The other women agreed that Hypsipyle was being prudent and far sighted. But Polyxo was of a different opinion.

"Your majesty," she said. "I raised you not on milk alone, but on my counsels. You always listened to me when you were a child, and now you have grown up and are the queen you still pay heed to me from time to time because you find my thinking wise and reasonable. And you, too, women of Lemnos, hear my words; for though the years may now weigh heavily upon my shoulders, they have taught me to distinguish right from wrong. And it is a mistake to refuse admittance to these men who may, for all we know, have been sent us by the gods themselves. We must not only welcome them ashore, but try to keep them with us for all time. Do you not see that our race is doomed to extinction without the men we need to give us children? How can you let such splendid fellows stand before you and yet still wish to turn them away? Are you not convinced by now that they are nothing like the men that once we knew? Invite them to disembark at once. Ask them to come into our city, and receive them not like passing strangers but as your husbands, to protect you with their love and sow the seeds of a new generation that will bring wealth and happiness to our island."

Polyxo's wise words fell on willing ears, and Hypsipyle echoed the feelings of all the women when she walked up to the ship and called:

"You are free to come ashore and enter our city. We shall receive you all with joy, and together we shall celebrate our decision to allow men on our island once again."

The Argonauts came happily ashore and set off for the city with the women. Only Heracles remained on board the Argo. His grief for the children whose death still stained his hands and his determination to win absolution for his foul deed by sacrifices and self-denial would not allow him to join his comrades while they dallied with the women of Lemnos.

Meanwhile, the heroes were being made welcome at the palace of Hypsipyle, where a feast had begun which looked as if it would never come to an end. Night and day they frolicked with the Lemnian women, and so delighted were they with the unexpected attentions they were receiving that they were in no mood to return to the Argo. Besides, had they wanted to leave, the women would not let them. Hypsipyle, who by now had fallen in love with Jason, spoke to him quite openly.

"We did not wish to let you come ashore at first," she told him, "but now we do not want to let you go. These few days we have known you, have been enough to make us love you all. We want you to stay for ever on our island, to give us children and start families. Besides, I can't deny that we are in real need of your protection, strength and skills, for we have many powerful enemies. And last of all I wish to tell you this: you can be sure that if we have men who treat us honestly and frankly, we shall treat them ten times better in our turn."

Of course, the Argonauts could not agree to stay on Lemnos for ever, so they avoided saying 'yes'. On the other hand, they were having such a good time that they could not bring themselves to say 'no' either! And so the days rolled by, and not a single member of the crew had any thought of returning to the ship. And worst of all: the more Lemnos grew on them, the more tiresome the memory of the golden fleece became, and more tiresome still when they recalled their backbreaking hours at the oars, and the dangers that lay in wait for them on their voyage into the unknown.

Was their brave quest destined to be forgotten so easily, then? Was the flame which had been lit within their hearts to be blown out within so short a space? Was there no-one to remind them who they were, and what they had set themselves to achieve, before it was too late? Fortunately, there was such a man. It was Heracles, who had been waiting patiently on board all these days till finally, his patience coming to an end, he sprang ashore and came running to the city.

The Argonauts were eating and drinking and making merry with their women at the palace of Hypsipyle when the doors burst open like a thunderclap and the great hero came storming in!

A frozen silence descended on the great hall. Heracles looked down on his comrades in amazement, as they lay there, heads bowed in shame. Then suddenly his wrath erupted.

"Shame on you!" he roared, "and shame on me for agreeing to come with you! Is this the noble aim you agreed to risk your lives for? Is this why you left your homes, your fathers,

..."Shame on you!" he roared, "and shame on me for agreeing to come with you!"...

wives and children? Where are the noble dreams that fired your hearts? And what will men say of us tomorrow when they learn that we exchanged the difficulties and dangers that were set before us for soft comforts and idle pleasures? What will they say of you, Jason, knowing that you gave your promise to achieve the most impossible and noble feat ever attempted by any man on earth? What will they say of you, Theseus, who once risked your life to kill the Minotaur and save the children of Athens? What will they say of you, Idas, who did not hesitate to pitch your strength against a god? What will they say of all you who have so many glorious deeds to your credit? Well, let me tell you. They will say you all received the name of hero by mistake. They will say that you cowered like dogs in the face of danger and have now revealed your real selves!"

"Enough, Heracles! Kill us one by one, but do not humiliate us so. Come on, men! Back to the Argo! Up! The golden fleece awaits!"

The voice of command was that of Jason, who had changed back in a moment from Hypsipyle's lover into the bold commander of the Argonauts.

Pushing their plates aside, the whole crew sprang to their feet and ran outside. The startled women could not understand how everything had changed so suddenly. With tears streaming down their faces, they begged the men to stay. Hypsipyle pleaded with Jason to remain on Lemnos and be king. But to no avail. The heroes marched down to the Argo deaf to all entreaties. And they would even have left without thinking to take any supplies with them had not some women come running at the last minute to bring them food and water. Quickly, they all jumped on board and cast loose. Tiphys took his place at the tiller while the others bent to the oars, and the Argo pulled out of harbour to the sound of bitter wailing. The island women had good reason to mourn the Argonauts' departure: not only had they loved these men, but they knew that as a result of this brief encounter they would bear children who would never see their fathers. For now it was all over and the Argo was drawing fast away from Lemnos.

After a few days' sailing, the Argonauts found themselves approaching the Hellespont. Before passing through the straits, Jason decided it would be wise to call in at the neighbouring island of Imbros to learn if they were likely to encounter any dangers.

It proved a sound decision, for there they were informed that king Laomedon of Troy refused to allow any foreign ship to enter the Hellespont.

"We must be prepared to fight if need be," said Jason to his comrades.

"Do that and you are doomed," an old islander replied. "Laomedon has set a whole fleet to guard the straits. There is no way you can get through."

Here Lynceus showed himself even more decisive than his captain.

"It's very simple," he said. "We shall pass through in the night. There is no moon, and tonight we have a cloudy sky. It will be so dark that we shall make our passage up the narrows without being seen at all."

"And how do you hope to find your way when you can't see a thing?" retorted the old man. "Besides, the narrows are so long that even if you could make out where you were going it would be impossible to get through before dawn; and if you row too quickly through the darkness, then you'll smash your ship upon the rocks, for sure."

But Lynceus knew that there was no such danger.

"We shall steer clear of the rocks, be certain of that," he told the old man, giving Jason a meaningful glance. And Jason, who knew just what he meant, decided that they would make their way up the Hellespont in the dead of night.

"Yet there is a danger," Heracles reminded them. "We

must be sure that we are out the oth
breaks. I think we can make it, don't yo
searching look at his comrades.

"Of course!" they all replied spontaneo

The heroes set off. By the time they ha ...ed the straits, night had already fallen. They could see nothing before them, not even where the entrance lay. But Lynceus' keen eyes could distinguish it clearly.

Without waiting on Jason's orders, he went and took his post at Tiphys' side, shouting:

"Pull on the oars with all your might, and we shall make it. There are no obstacles ahead."

"We shall make it!" Heracles cried back, putting all his formidable strength behind his oar. The others followed his example, and the Argo shot forward with unaccustomed speed as Lynceus showed Tiphys the way through the pitch blackness.

After a while he shouted:

"We have entered the straits. From now on we face Laomedon's ships, but they cannot see us. All we need is strength behind those oars."

The Argo shot through the narrows like a streak of lightning. The heroes rowed on tirelessly with all their might, and thanks to Lynceus' sharp eyes, the Argonauts' vessel ayed well away from rocks and enemy ships.

All through the night the crew bent relentlessly to their oars, until Lynceus cried out:

"I can see the end of it!"

With enthusiastic cheers and renewed powers, the heroes brought the Argo out into the broad sea. When at last it dawned they were many miles away, and no enemy vessel could be seen in their vicinity.

So the Argonauts passed through the Hellespont, even though it was guarded by a powerful fleet. And all this was due to Lynceus, who got his name because his eyes were as keen as those of a lynx, the wild cat which can see through the thickest darkness.

The heroes continued their voyage helped on by the wind. Now they were in the second of the three seas, and what they needed above all was a quiet anchorage where they might rest a while.

To starboard the coastline could be seen, and before them lay a promontory which resembled a mountain rising from the sea. A thin rocky neck linked it to the mainland, forming a natural harbour.

"Let us cast anchor here," suggested Tiphys. "The mountain will protect us from the wind, and we shall be able to find a safe shelter for the Argo."

They all agreed, and when they drew nearer they saw that they were not only in a protected harbour, but near a city, too.

Having tied the Argo up, they stepped out on the shore, where they were greeted warmly by the inhabitants of the city, who were known as Dolionians and were a hard-working and hospitable people. As luck would have it, their young king Cyzicus was to be married that very day, and a great feast would be held. The strangers were invited, too, and Cyzicus placed Jason at his side. All the Argonauts were present except Heracles, who once more stayed on board the ship.

"You have chanced upon us on a happy day," said Cyzicus, "and perhaps you are thinking that our life is always as pleasant as this. It could indeed be, for our land is fertile and we are an industrious people. But unluckily for us we have two powerful enemies who will not leave us to enjoy the fruits of our labour. Up on that mountain which you see, there lives a tribe of fearsome giants, each of whom has six hands, and just to amuse themselves they toss huge rocks down on us, though we do nothing to provoke them. And as if the giants were not enough we have the Pelasgians, who are forever making raids on us, to loot us of our wealth."

Cyzicus had hardly finished speaking when the horrible monsters he had described appeared on the high rocks which overlooked the city. As soon as they set eyes on the Argo, they started hurling boulders to send her to the bottom. But Heracles, although he was alone on board, succeeded in saving the ship. Seizing his bow, he took aim at the giants one by one. Not one of the hero's arrows missed its mark. Several of them fell tumbling dead into the sea, while the others were forced to withdraw for safety to a spot from which they could not harm the ship. In the meantime, however, the Argonauts had launched another attack from the landward side. They killed a number of them and forced the others back up to the summit of the rocks, where Heracles' arrows awaited them once more. In the end, not a single giant escaped and the Dolionians could not find words to thank the heroes for delivering them from the attacks of these fearsome creatures.

When the time for their departure came, they showered so many gifts upon them and offered so much in the way of provisions that it was a problem finding cargo space for it all. In return, the Argonauts made them a gift of their anchor-stone, having first carved another, larger one. Centuries later, the descendants of the Dolionians were still showing it to travellers as proof that the famous Argonauts had once passed their way.

As soon as the Argo put out from the harbour of the hospitable Dolionians, she ran into a severe storm. Conditions worsened during the night and carried the ship this way and that. Finally, with the help of Lynceus, Tiphys managed to bring her into sheltered waters where they tied up for the night. Without realising it, however, they had made a complete circle of the promontory and cast anchor on the other side of the neck which linked it to the mainland. In the darkness, they were unable to make out the features of the place. Even Lynceus, to whom it somehow looked familiar, dismissed the thought because, like all the others, he believed they must by now be far, far away from their friends of yesterday.

The Dolionians in their turn, who could never have imagined that the Argonauts had sailed back, and who were frequently troubled by night-time raids from the Pelasgians, threw themselves on the supposed invaders in an effort to expel them.

A blind struggle now broke out, and the Argonauts, few as they were, might have inflicted severe casualties on the Dolionians had they not been shielded by the darkness. As it was, only Jason was certain that he had killed one of their attackers, and possibly their chief, as he had been riding in a chariot. The skirmish continued for some hours, until dawn began to break, when suddenly one of the Dolionians cried out:

"Put down your arms! We are fighting with our friends!"

The combat ceased at once, and expressions of remorse came over the faces of the opposing forces when they saw against whom they had been battling. A moment later, these turned to groans of dismay when they saw that the only casualty of the night's skirmish was king Cyzicus the handsome, brave young man who but hours before had been celebrating the happiest day of his whole life. Yet this evil morning was to see more than the death of Cyzicus alone. Anxious for her husband, his young wife, the lovely Cleite, ran in search of him; and when she found him lying there, fell on his lifeless body with a heart-rending cry. Cleite never rose again from that spot. She died of sorrow at her husband's pointless death. Now yesterday's bride and groom both lay dead and the joy of the day before was turned to tragedy and grief.

Cyzicus and Cleite were buried amid the general mourning of the Dolionians, while the Argonauts stood by in wordless sorrow. The next day they honoured the dead with funeral games in which all the Argonauts won the

... the remorse turned to groans of dismay when they saw that the only casualty of the night's skirmish was king Cyzicus...

admiration of the Dolionians for their prowess.

With heavy hearts, the heroes left Cyzicus, as the city was henceforth to be known, and as they set off, Jason proposed a rowing race in honour of those who had perished.

"I don't see how we can have a race when we're all aboard the same ship," objected Polydeuces.

"There is a way," said Heracles. "We shall all pull together, and those who hold out longest will be the victors. We shall divide ourselves into two teams: those on the right and those on the left – and we shall appoint a committee to decide which of the two is better."

Soon the race began. Given their stroke by the notes of Orpheus' lyre the oarsmen drove the Argo swiftly forward. For a long time the vessel cut through the sea in a perfectly straight line which meant that both teams were of equal strength; but eventually the moment came when the ship began to veer to one side, proving that one team was now pulling more powerfully and the other team had tired. Then the judges declared the winners. It was the team which included Heracles and Jason.

"Now the winning team will divide itself in two," said Heracles, "and we shall continue."

"Castor and Polydeuces will join you," the judges decided. "They are the strongest members of the losing team."

Everyone accepted the judges' ruling and the race began again. And so it went on till in the end there were only two pairs left: Heracles and Jason pulling on one side, and Castor and Polydeuces on the other.

The two brothers made a desperate effort to keep the Argo on a straight course, but they could not maintain the pace for long. It was clear that Castor was down to the last ounce of his strength. He was not prepared to admit defeat, however, and with a superhuman effort managed to keep pulling strongly at his oar. Even so, the Argo began to slip slightly off true, since Heracles and Jason possessed still greater energy. Seeing his brother trying to maintain a struggle that was beyond his powers, Polydeuces felt a mixture of pity and sorrow. He pretended that he, too, could keep up the unequal contest no longer, and pulled less strongly. And as the Argo slid sharply round to one side he let the oar slip from his hands. What did it matter whether he took the third place or the fourth, since anyway the other two still had reserves of power, and it was obvious that he could not compete with either of them? Utterly exhausted, Castor too released his grip upon the oar. Now he realised why Polydeuces had given up the race. "Would I ever be able to do that for my brother?" he asked himself, and hung his head in shame.

When the two Dioscuri had withdrawn, Jason and Heracles went into the last round of the contest, stubbornly continuing to push the Argo through the water though only the two of them were left. Streaming with sweat, they lunged forward and then dragged back the oars. It was clear that Heracles had a lot of distance in him yet, while Jason drew his strength from one source only: his determination to defeat the mighty hero. For hours the two of them rowed on alone. Jason's stubborn willpower lent him wings. All marvelled at his powers of endurance. But to beat Heracles? No, that was impossible. Nobody could pull off such a coup – and neither could Jason. In the end he was so utterly drained that he could go on no longer and let the oar drop from his hands.

"Tiphys!" bellowed Heracles. "Hang onto the rudder and keep the Argo on a straight course!" And then the mighty hero kept up the contest, although he had already won. Now he needed to exert twice the power to keep the Argo moving, but the tireless hero found it somehow. The oar grated against the rowlock and bent back like a bow as Heracles' fearsome strength was exerted against it, and still the Argo kept moving forward. All things have a breaking point. It was not Heracles who had reached his limit, though, but the oar, which suddenly broke in two. The hero looked down sorrowfully at the stump which remained in his hands, then tossed it into the sea in disgust.

"Jason!" he shouted. "We must anchor somewhere to cut another oar."

"We need water, too," said Jason. "After all the sweat we've lost, we've almost drunk the barrel dry. Lynceus! Find us a suitable anchorage. It's time for us to have a little rest."

Lynceus' hawk-like eyes were not slow to pick out a stretch of coast with abundant vegetation where they would be able to find not only water but a straight-trunked tree they could use to replace the broken oar. Tiphys turned the Argo in the direction Lynceus indicated and soon the Argonauts sailed into a peaceful little harbour. They had landed on the coast of Mysia.

When the heroes had eaten and rested on the sand, Heracles got up and told his young squire Hylas:

"Bring a pitcher and let's go. You look for water, and I'll search for a tree."

They set off together, but soon their ways parted. Hylas had to go in one direction for the water and Heracles in another for the tree.

"Don't wait for me," the mighty hero said to Hylas. "As

soon as you have filled your pitcher, go straight back to the shore. I shall have to climb up the mountain to get my new oar, and I'll take longer than you."

Indeed, Heracles had to go quite high before he found a fir tree which was ideal for his purpose. He soon brought it down, trimmed off the branches, then hoisted it on his shoulder to take it back to where the ship lay and carve it into an oar. On arriving at the shore, however, he was surprised to learn that young Hylas had not yet returned. After some time had gone by, he grew anxious and decided to go in search of him.

The hero loved this boy like his own son. He had adopted him after the lad lost his father and he his own children. Good-natured, willing and handsome, Hylas had won the affection of everyone on board.

"I'll come with you to search for Hylas," said Polyphemus, the hero from Thessaly, and the two of them set off at once with worried faces.

They searched in every place imaginable, but Hylas was nowhere to be found. All they came across was his pitcher, standing on the shore of a quiet pool in a deep gorge.

"Hylas! Hylas! Hylas!" they started to shout; but all that came back was the echo of their own voices: "Hylas! Hylas! Hylas!" and nothing more.

They searched for endless hours, but all in vain, for where Hylas was now, not only could he not be found but neither could he answer to their call. Where was the young man, indeed? And what had befallen him?

No evil fate had overtaken him. He had only stumbled into an adventure as pleasant as it was unhoped-for.

On reaching the pool where Heracles and Polyphemus had found the pitcher, he had been so enchanted by the peace and beauty of the spot that he was in no hurry to fill his jar and leave. Bewitched, he bent and gazed into its waters, which were deep and clear as crystal. He saw the waterplants, the rocks and caves, the little multicoloured fish and the other delightful things that are only to be found in lakes and rivers. What he did not see was the two eyes that gazed up at him from the green depths. He did not glimpse the nymph Dryope, who was hidden behind the plants which clung to the rocks. And the longer Hylas knelt and gazed at all that beauty, the more admiringly did she gaze at him. She marvelled at his golden hair, the blueness of his eyes, his well-shaped lips and lithe young body. Enchanted by his looks, she fell in love with him immediately.

Then Hylas bent to sip a little water, not so much out of thirst but to luxuriate in all that cool freshness that spread itself around him. An intoxicating thrill of pleasure ran through his body as his lips touched the surface of the lake. As if some goddess had bestowed a kiss upon him, he lost all sense of the world around and as in some languorous dream abandoned himself to the touch of the limpid waters. As he did so, two milkwhite arms rose from the surface of the pool and pulled him down in their sweet embrace. They were the arms of Dryope, calling him to live for ever with her in their depths.

Before he could even register surprise, Hylas found himself in the kingdom of the water-nymphs. Dryope's lovely sister-nymphs came in joyful haste and led the young couple to an enchanting cave, and there, beneath the water, the ecstatic Hylas was married to the beautiful Dryope. Yet there came a moment when familiar voices crying "Hylas! Hylas! Hylas!" reminded him that he had left his dear comrades up above and that now they were searching for him anxiously. His heart tightened in his breast, but just as nymphs cannot speak to mortals from beneath the water, neither could Hylas tell his companions where he could be found, and how happy he now was.

So Hylas' friends lost him for ever, and he remained in Mysia ever after. Indeed, the people of those parts say that Hylas still lives in the lakes and rivers there and has be-

... Before he could even register surprise, Hylas found himself in the kingdom of the water-nymphs...

come immortal. They even say that each year in neighbouring Prusa, a sacrifice was made to him. The priest would shout his name out loud three times and the people would call back three times in return, as if echoing the priest's voice. Finally, they would all scatter through the forest and pretend to search for the lost youth, crying "Hylas! Hylas! Hylas!" In this way, the memory of Dryope's beloved was kept alive, just as the passing of Heracles and the Argonauts was never forgotten in those regions.

Meanwhile, Heracles and Polyphemus were continuing their search, unable to fathom what could have happened to Hylas. They scoured the forest tirelessly all day, but when night fell they lost hope and decided to return. They, too, went astray in the darkness and did not realise they were heading in the opposite direction to the one they should have taken. In the morning they saw that they were far from the shore, but still they did not know which way they ought to follow, until Hermes, messenger of Zeus, appeared before them. After reassuring them that Hylas was now living happily in the watery kingdom of the nymphs, where they would never find him, he added:

"It is the will of Zeus that you do not rejoin your companions. You, Polyphemus, must wait till night falls again.

Then, when you see in which quarter of the horizon the constellation of Crius appears, you must head in that direction. When you reach the sea you will find a natural harbour sheltered by a tall hill. Show this place to the local people and call on them to help you build a city there. They will hear your voice, and then you shall raise a city on that spot which you shall call Crius and of which you shall be king. And now you, Heracles, son of Zeus, listen in your turn."

"I know myself to be the son of Amphitryon and Alcmene," Heracles replied. "Why do you call me son of Zeus?"

"You are the son of Zeus – and yet your life has been filled with pain and suffering and will continue so. Your father's decision (or rather, our father's, since you are my brother) is that you return to Greece. There, you will have to suffer torture and humiliation and place your life in danger many times, but you will perform more and greater labours than the world has ever seen before. And while all tyrants will cringe before your strength and long for your destruction, you will be loved so much by common men that the gods themselves will envy your renown. Set forth, therefore, on the road which mighty Zeus has laid down for you, and do not be troubled about your companions."

This said, Hermes saluted them with a raised hand, wrapped himself in a cloud and disappeared from sight.

Staggered though they were, the two friends had no choice but to obey. Heracles, however, was in no hurry to set off for Greece immediately. First he wished to help Polyphemus with the building of Crius, which became a fair city and is known today as Kios.

The Argonauts waited patiently for their missing comrades until a wind blew up from landwards. Then Jason ordered them all on board the Argo and they set sail.

"We can wait for them no longer," he said, "and nor shall we send out any more of our comrades to be lost in these unknown, menacing regions."

The Argonauts left with heavy hearts and the voyage continued in silence. All the crew were sad and thoughtful. So gloomy was the atmosphere aboard that in the end Jason stood up and said:

"We have lost our friends, but that does not mean we must bewail our fate the whole voyage through. Orpheus, take your lyre and bring some joy and life back to the Argo!"

But Telamon, who had been Heracles' most faithful friend, did not approve of this. He rose angrily and shouted:

"Shame on you, Jason! Is that all it means to you, then?

We have lost three of our comrades, and to you it's as if nothing had happened. Ah, now I understand. You're glad that Heracles is gone! Yes, that's it! You were afraid he would steal all your glory, and that's why you forced us to set sail in such a hurry! Well, I'm not going any further! Tiphys, turn the Argo round! Come on! Let's go back and search for our lost companions!"

"Telamon!" warned Jason, "I give the orders on this ship! The Argo will not change course!"

But ignoring Jason, Telamon threw himself on Tiphys, pushed him roughly aside, seized the tiller and heaved the ship round in a sharp turn. However, this clumsy manoeuvre almost brought disaster. As the Argo turned, the wind caught the sail from the side and made the vessel heel over so far that it would have sunk had a god not sprung up from the waves to hold it. It was Glaucus, the protector of sailors, who had risen from a humble fisherman to become a sea-god and a seer.

"You shall not return!" he roared in his hoarse voice. "It was the will of the father of gods and men that your comrades should stay behind in Mysia. You need not be anxious on their behalf, for no harm has come to them. Keep onwards as one man, and never for a moment lose sight of your goal: the golden fleece!"

With these words Glaucus swung the Argo all alone back onto her correct course, and giving her a mighty shove sent her swiftly on her way.

Telamon immediately apologised to Jason and the other heroes; then Orpheus struck a chord from his lyre, and the quarrel which had broken out on board the Argo was quickly forgotten in song.

Having sailed on for a great distance, they saw a city on the shores of Bithynia and decided to call in there as they were running low on provisions. As soon as they came ashore, they saw a spring and went to take water. But when they drew near they heard a voice behind them:

"Get away from that spring! We don't give our water away that easily to everyone who comes along!"

Turning, they saw a man tall as a giant. His face was savage and he looked a heartless brute. He was surrounded by armed men. The Argonauts stayed where they were, frozen with surprise. The stranger swaggered up to them, examined each one with a haughty air, then said:

"We have a custom here. It may seem barbarous to you, but we find it very entertaining. When foreigners come this way, we tell them that if they want to drink the water from our well, one of them will have to box me for it – and then I punch him to death, whoever he is. So choose your best boxer, and as soon as I have killed him you may take all the water you want. I may add that your drinks will be cheap at the price, for this spring which you see was a gift to me from my father, earth-shaker Poseidon himself. Now let me introduce myself: I am Amycus, king of the Bebrycans and the terror of all the neighbouring peoples!"

The Argonauts' hearts sank when they heard his words. But one of them sprang forward bravely. It was Polydeuces.

"I will take you on!" he challenged.

Polydeuces was a splendid boxer, and no-one in the whole of Greece had a harder punch than he, but it still seemed a hopelessly unequal contest. Castor tried to dissuade his brother, but to no avail. Meanwhile Amycus was looking Polydeuces up and down in scorn, for he was young, short of stature and not an impressive sight at all.

"I didn't ask to fight with someone who is tired of life," he said ironically, "but with someone who believes that he can kill me."

Polydeuces paid him back in the same coin. Without even looking at Amycus he said to the Argonauts:

"Let him talk, the gasbag. He'll soon run out of hot air."

"I see the brat is insolent as well," snarled Amycus. "All

right, if that's what you want. But bid farewell to your comrades first, because you'll be taking a little trip to the underworld quite soon!"

"Leave off your bragging and let's get on with it," was Polydeuces' curt reply.

They quickly tied on their gloves, and Amycus strutted around the ring throwing punches in the air for everyone to admire. Polydeuces, on the other hand, looked grave and thoughtful, for he saw that he was up against a difficult problem: only if he could strike Amycus on the head did he stand any chance of winning – but his opponent stood so tall it would be difficult to reach there. "The only way is to tire him first," said Polydeuces to himself.

The match began and Amycus swung to the attack. His plan was to lay Polydeuces out with a blow to the head and then finish him off. Putting all his fearsome strength into his punch, he went straight for the young man's jaw. But instead of connecting, his blow fell on thin air and he nearly put his shoulder out. He had never guessed his opponent was so nimble, and was taken completely by surprise when he ducked with such speed. He launched another blow, but this fared no better than the first. Now the giant grew savage and threw even heavier punches. All in vain; Polydeuces was so light on his feet that he either feinted past these attacks or warded them off with his knuckles. Amycus went wild with rage and started flailing madly, counting on the one blow that might find its target and leave his opponent dizzy enough for a couple more punches to finish him off. But this tactic did not bring the desired result either, and Amycus then began to realise what kind of fighter he was up against – especially when Polydeuces began slipping in sudden lightning blows which struck home with all the force of steel. Worst of all, as the minutes went by his enemy became ever more formidable while he became slower and more lumbering. Soon he was in a cold sweat of fear at the realisation that his powers had ebbed away and his opponent was still fresh and full of fight. "It's lucky I'm tall and he can't reach my head," Amycus thought. "I must watch out for my stomach, though." At that very instant, a sledgehammer blow from Polydeuces slashed right through the giant's guard and struck him where he had most feared: full in the midriff. He doubled up in agony, offering his head as a perfect target for Polydeuces' fist – and received a stunning reminder that there were stronger punches in the world than his. If the blow had landed on his temple it would have killed him outright, but even as it was he was completely incapable of continuing the fight. He fell to his knees on the ground, his arms limp and useless at his side. Polydeuces glared down at him with savage hatred, and from the look in his eyes Amycus knew that his end had come.

"Mercy!" he gasped, with what little breath was left in him.

"Mercy? When did you ever show any?" Polydeuces snarled in fury.

"Mercy!" the giant cried again, and seeing there was no other hope, he dragged himself over to Polydeuces and kissed his feet.

But this act only heaped fuel on the young man's furious scorn.

"Worm!" he roared. "Answer me when I speak to you!" And savagely grinding his fist into Amycus' face, he repeated his question:

"Answer me: when did you ever show pity for your innocent victims?"

"Spare my life, and I shall give you all the gold you want!"

"I didn't fight for gold – just for a drink of water! You deserve to die but I cannot bring myself to kill a creature that crawls at my feet. Here's how you can save yourself, though: swear by Poseidon, whom you claim to be your father, that you will never again lay a finger on any stranger

... You deserve to die but I cannot bring myself to kill a creature that crawls at my feet...

who asks you for food and water!"

The trembling Amycus gave this solemn promise. Then he ordered his men to bring provisions and rich gifts for all the Argonauts; and when they had also filled their pitchers with spring water, they bid them a fair voyage. Amycus kept his vow. He had been given such a lesson, that no stranger would ever again be in any danger in the land of the Bebrycans.

The Argonauts' last port of call before leaving the sea of Marmara was on its northern coast, at a little harbour where there was a small city. The harbour was protected by a hill, on which the palace and fortress were built. Zetes and Calais, the two winged sons of Boreas, were familiar with this place. Its name was Salmydessus, and it stood on the eastern coast of Thrace.

"This city is ruled by Phineus, who married our sister Cleopatra," they said. "He is a great seer, and the only mortal from whom the gods do not conceal their secrets. We must go and see him. He will give us valuable advice about our mission."

The Argonauts disembarked and went into the city, but they were struck by its air of desolation and abandonment. Its streets were deserted, and worse still, the whole place was foul with bird-droppings. Unable to guess what could have happened here, the Argonauts decided to go up to the acropolis above the town and call at the palace.

When they reached the top of the hill they found a palace with broken doors and windows; even the roof was half in ruins. But strangest of all, the bird-droppings which had filled the town were even thicker here and covered the rooms, the corridors and every other surface. When they went into the great hall, they received their greatest and most awful shock of all: seated at a great wooden table, amid a sea of filth whose stench caught at their throats, was an old, old man. His skin clung to his bones, his clothes were spattered with excrement, and where his eyes had been there were only sunken hollows. Not even Zetes and Calais could bring themselves to believe that this was Phineus, the darling of the gods. They all felt a rush of pity for the unfortunate old man, and Jason asked him who he was and how he came to be in such a hopeless state.

"I am Phineus, king of Salmydessus," the blind man began. "This was once a fair and wealthy city, but now it lies in ruins and I have sunk to the misery in which you see me. Once there was a time when the gods loved me so much that they not only gave me the daughter of Boreas in marriage but would often invite me to Olympus, where I ate and drank with them in their golden palaces. They spoke to me quite openly, and told me of their troubles and their joys and even revealed their secrets to me, as if I, too, were immortal. But I had not ceased to be a common man and I pitied my fellow-beings even when they were pursued by the wrath of the gods. Sometimes, to help them, I would reveal certain information that I had learned from the Olympians. When mighty Zeus and the other gods became aware of this, so terrible was their anger that they decided on a harsh punishment for me. Thus it was that I, Phineus, who had dined at the tables of the immortals, suddenly found myself hated by those who live on Olympus more bitterly than any man on earth. First they took away my sight. Then Zeus whipped up a terrible storm, filled with thunder and lightning, which destroyed my palace in one night. Last of all, as if my sufferings were not great enough already, he sent two Harpies, winged monsters who have turned my life into an endless torture. Whenever I sit at table they come to snatch my food, leaving only enough to ensure that my long martyrdom goes on, and then they defile everything with their droppings, even the plate I eat from. Hunger can be borne, but the filth with which they have filled this place is beyond all enduring. That is why everyone has fled from Salmydessus and I am left alone to bear my punishment. It is hard indeed to suffer misfortunes such as mine, but a hundred times harder when one has sunk from high estate."

All the Argonauts were filled with pity for Phineus, especially the sons of Boreas, for this man had been their sister's husband. Something had to be done to help him. They had food with them, which they set down on the table for the unlucky old man to eat; but he had not even carried the first morsel to his mouth when the fearsome Harpies appeared. They were strange creatures, like women from the middle up and the rest of them like birds. They swooped in through a gaping hole in the half-shattered roof, hovered above Phineus, and in an instant had gobbled all the food which had been placed before him. Then they fouled his plate, the table and the whole great chamber with their droppings, leaving a stench which was more than could be borne.

Zetes and Calais, the two winged sons of Boreas, sprang to their feet in an instant. Drawing their swords, they unfolded their great wings and launched themselves upon the Harpies. The monsters soared into the sky in terror, but the two brothers pursued them. And the faster they flew away, the harder the Boreades came after them. They crossed over land and sea, winged their way across Greece

and all the Peloponnese and came at last, exhausted, to some tiny islands below Zacynthos where the two brothers caught up with them. Just as they were about to pierce the Harpies with their swords, the creatures let out a desperate cry for divine help and the goddess Iris appeared to order the sons of Boreas not to kill them. Only when the Harpies had promised never to trouble Phineus again did the two brothers accede to her command and leave them unharmed

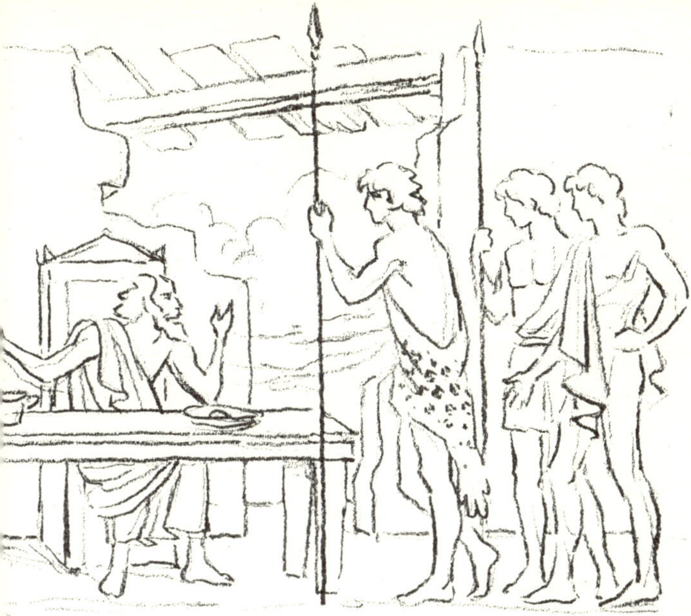

on those islets. They have been called in Greek the Strophades or "turning" islands ever since, for it was here that Zetes and Calais turned in their flight and went back to their companions.

So Phineus was delivered from the Harpies; and to show his gratitude to the Argonauts he decided to give them information and advice which would be precious on their voyage.

"I know who you are and where you are bound for," he told them. "I have been waiting patiently, years now, for you to come. Seer that I am, I knew that one day my sufferings would be ended by the Argonauts, when they passed by here on their way to Colchis, to win the golden fleece."

The heroes stared at Phineus wide-eyed as he continued:

It is a noble mission you are on but a very hard one; and soon, not very far from here, you will encounter an obstacle which may well prove beyond your powers to overcome. This is the Symplegades, two tall rocks which bar the way out of these waters and prevent any ship from reaching the great broad sea on whose farthest shore lies Colchis. They close and open so unexpectedly that any ship which tries to sail between them is certain to be crushed. But fear not, you will make the passage unscathed, – if you follow my instructions and are aided by the gods and your own strong arms. Now listen to what you must do: approach the rocks, but stand off at a safe distance. Then, as soon as you see them opening, release a dove. If it succeeds in flying past unharmed, then, when they next open, you will pass through, too. But if the dove is crushed between the rocks, that means that you have no choice but to return the way you came. For if you then decide to risk the passage, the

Argo will be smashed to matchwood, and you will all be killed."

The Argonauts were troubled by this news, and when they had reembarked on the Argo they sailed on in the hope that the Symplegades were only the imaginings of a blind old man whose mind had been turned by the tortures he had suffered. However, shortly afterwards, something very strange caught their attention.

While the sky was clear and cloudless, they could hear thunder in the East. As they sailed on, the thunderclaps grew louder and then louder still. And yet there was not a single cloud in the sky. When they came nearer yet, the sound became more easy to distinguish: it was a thunderous roar, repeated at irregular intervals. The Argonauts could not make out where this strange noise was coming from, until Lynceus cried:

"We are approaching the Symplegades! They are hidden in the haze on the horizon, but they will soon show clearer."

Indeed, the two gigantic moving rocks soon became visible. The roar they made as they crashed together rapidly grew ear-splitting, and now that the Argonauts had drawn close enough to see every detail, they stood in silent awe before this fearsome but majestic spectacle. As they watched, the two rocks, huge as mountains, rushed towards each other with dizzying speed and collided with a crash that made them think a hundred thunderclaps and bolts of lightning had struck the earth together. As they did so, a huge cloud rose above the water. It was the spray from the collision, which shot into the sky and momentarily concealed everything from view. As it rose, so the sea boiled and churned. Not even the trident of earth-shaker Poseidon in his greatest hour of wrath could have stirred up such commotion. What Phineus had warned them of was nothing to what they now beheld.

In the meantime, the Argo had reached a point beyond which it would be dangerous to proceed. It seemed sheer madness to launch themselves into that boiling hell, yet none of the heroes suggested they retreat. At that desperate moment, Jason remembered the words of the goddess Hera: "Go forward, Jason, and I shall be at your side". So he took a dove out of its cage, and first looking his comrades straight in the eyes, and seeing the determination written there, he released the bird from his enfolding hands. The rocks were just about to open. The dove shot forward like an arrow, but the gap was narrow and in a moment they began to move and close again. The terrified dove flew faster still to escape its fate, but in those last few seconds the outcome was unsure.

"The rocks have crushed it!" groaned Tiphys in despair.

"No, the dove is through!" cried Lynceus.

"It's through!" they all cried, unable to conceal their relief.

And indeed it had got through. But even so the great stones managed to close upon its tail, and two white feathers fluttered for a moment in the air before they were lost in the spray which boiled up from the sea after that earth-shaking collision.

"Ready?" shouted Jason, the moment the rocks drew open once again. "Forward!"

The heroes bent to the oars as if possessed, and the Argo surged towards the gap; but soon they found themselves in seas so wild that their vessel was tossed in all directions like a cork. For all this, they somehow found the strength to keep her head into the wind, but then the Argo suddenly changed course. No longer obedient to Tiphys' hand upon the tiller, shc began to spin in a circle. They had fallen into a huge whirlpool, which was rapidly sucking the ship towards its eye, where a vast black gulf lay eager to devour them. All hope seemed gone, and the abyss was about to swallow up the Argo, when some unseen power suddenly dragged her away from the lip of the maelstrom and shot her into the narrow gap between the rocks! As the Argonauts let out their pent breath in relief, a woman's voice called out:

"Jason, you helped me once. It was time that I repaid you." The voice had come from the wooden figurehead. The goddess Hera had not forgotten him.

The heroes bent to their oars with strength renewed, and the Argo sped between the Symplegades like a streak of lightning. As it did, the towering rocks closed in to crush them from both sides. They had just got through when, with a thunderous crash, the great stones closed together, a second too late to catch the Argo, but not too late to nip the tail end of her stern and splinter the wooden decoration there. The Argonauts, like the dove, had been saved by a hair's breadth. Phineus had proved a powerful seer, and his help as valuable as that of Hera. As soon as the Argo had passed through, the Symplegades opened once again and did not close – for it was decreed by the Fates that if ever a ship succeeded in slipping through their clutches, they would remain wide open for all time. Thanks to their unflinching courage the Argonauts had achieved this seemingly impossible task. The sea lane to the East now lay open to all the generations yet to come.

... the Argo sped between the Symplegades like a streak of lightning...

The heroes now came into a vast and unknown sea, and no one knew how long their wanderings would continue before they reached their goal. Many rumours had reached their ears about these, distant parts. Somewhere along the route to Colchis, it was said, the river Thermodon flowed into the sea. On its banks lived the warlike Amazons, who fought on horseback and were feared by all the neighbouring tribes. Elsewhere lived the Chalybians, a race of skilled ironworkers who neither tilled the soil nor kept flocks but lived wholly on the product of their skills. Somewhere, too, in this region dwelt the Tibarenians, who left all manual labour to their womenfolk, while the men stayed at home with the children and occupied themselves with housework. The land of the Moesynoechians was also hereabouts. These were savage warriors who built tall wooden castles and fought with long spears and shields shaped like ivy-leaves. The Argonauts also knew that at some point beyond Colchis the titan Prometheus hung nailed to a rock, suffering the most hideous tortures ever inflicted upon god or mortal, and all for his love of mankind. But where exactly all these places lay, nobody could say, not even Lynceus, who could see behind the mountains.

At their first port of call in these new lands, the inhabitants greeted them warmly. The moment the Argonauts set foot on the shore, king Lycus, ruler of the land of Mariandyne, came running up to welcome them. When he learned that the strangers had beaten and humiliated his bitterest enemy, Amycus, he showered them with honours and laid on a feast which lasted many days. In parting, he presented them with ample stores and ordered his son Dascylus to go with them and guide them on their way.

Kindly though Lycus had received the Argonauts, the fates gave them a cruel welcome in these parts. While hunting, the seer Idmon was gored by a fearsome wild boar. Idas ran up with his spear and pinned the hideous monster to the earth. Then he lifted Idmon on his shoulders and carried him back to their comrades for his wound to be dressed, but so deeply had the boar's tusks pierced the hero that he died as he was being laid upon the ground.

"Idmon was a seer," said Idas, "and knew that he would die on this expedition. He told me so himself, but begged me not to reveal it to you before his death. He was a brave soul. Although he knew what fate awaited him, he did not wish to stay back and avoid it when all of us were setting out with such high hearts in search of the golden fleece."

But the death of plucky Idmon was not the only blow the Argonauts were dealt. Their splendid steersman, Tiphys, suddenly fell ill. His condition quickly worsened, and before the night was out they lost this comrade, too. Three days the heroes mourned their two dead friends, and when they had burned their bodies and placed the ashes in urns, they raised two earthen tomb-mounds in their memory, planting an upright oar upon the summit of each. Centuries later, the inhabitants of Mariandyne were still reverently showing strangers the oar-capped tombs where the two brave Argonauts lay buried.

Following the death of Tiphys, his place as helmsman was taken by Ancaeus of Samos, who proved himself in every way a worthy successor.

After a few more days at sea they put in at a city on the coast which they learned was named Sinope. Its people were hospitable and they got a friendly welcome. They had landed on a feast day, and at that very moment a sacrifice was being prepared. The ruler of the place invited the Argonauts to take part in the feast, and while thanking him, Jason asked in honour of which divinity the sacrifice was taking place. He was told that they were worshipping Sinope the nymph, daughter of the river-god Asopus.

"It seems you do not know the story of Sinope, even though she comes from your parts," said the ruler. "But now that you find yourselves among us, it is only proper that you should learn it." And he immediately called on a handsome young minstrel to recount to them in song how their city had come to be named after Sinope.

The minstrel came and sat amongst the Argonauts, struck a chord on his lyre and began to sing the myth of the daughter of Asopus.

"Sinope came to our land from distant Argos," went his song. "She was a nymph whose beauty put the sun itself to shade. Zeus saw her and fell madly in love; but Sinope was a shy and timid creature, and as soon as she set eyes on him she took to her heels in fright. Zeus pursued her, but she was as fleet and nimble as a wild goat and kept evading him. Night and day Zeus hunted down the lovely nymph, but it was not until Sinope reached this place, too tired to go on, that eventually he caught her. Even then he could not win her heart. He thought of offering her a gift, but did not know what would appease the trembling maiden, so in the end he decided to let her make the choice.

'Will you give me whatever I desire?' she asked him nervously.

'Anything you wish,' the impatient Zeus replied immediately. 'And rest assured, I never go back on my word.'

"Sinope's face lit up with joy and now she answered boldly, without hesitation: 'I want to stay a virgin for ever.'

"Zeus almost bit his tongue off in frustration, but there was nothing he could do about it now. So Sinope never married and lived here ever afterwards while we, to honour her, gave our city her name."

Amused by this charming tale, the Argonauts thanked the singer and his ruler. Then Orpheus took up his lyre and sang them songs of Greece, the fair land where the nymph Sinope had been born.

Orpheus moved all who heard him, but most deeply touched of all were three young men who came with tears in their eyes and said to the Argonauts: "We, too, are from Greece. The three of us are brothers and we came here with Heracles when he was searching for Hippolyta's belt; but one night we got lost and we have stayed here ever since. Now we want to come with you, aid you in your mission, and return with you to our homeland."

Jason and all the other Argonauts welcomed their three fellow-countrymen gladly. Now that some of the places at the oarsmen's benches stood empty, their assistance would be valuable. The three young men came from Tricca in Thessaly, and their names were Deilion, Autolycus and Phlogius.

The heroes put out to sea once more. They rowed

strongly, thrusting the Argo ever further from their beloved mother-country; yet there was no indication that they were approaching the goal of their long voyage. To starboard, sometimes near and sometimes far away, lay the coasts of unknown lands, while to their port the empty sea stretched endlessly away.

At last they reached a little island. Although it looked deserted, it stood so squarely in their course that they decided to make landfall there. They had not even secured the mooring-ropes, however, when one of the Argonauts, Oïleus by name, let out a cry of pain. An arrow stood quivering in his shoulder. Jason ran to help, and on pulling it out saw it was not an arrow but a heavy, pointed feather made of bronze. Fortunately, Oïleus was not seriously hurt, but a moment later another of these feathers embedded itself in the planking of the ship.

"Take cover under your shields and draw your bows!" Jason called out. "Be ready to repel the enemy!" But where was the enemy? They looked up and down the shore but saw nothing.

"There is no one hidden here," said Lynceus, whose piercing eyes could even see behind the rocks along the coastline, "only a bird, a huge one, in the sky above us. Watch out! Here come some more! It is they who are attacking us, and their feathers are of bronze, real arrows, like the ones that fell before. They are the same birds which Heracles once drove away from the lake of Stymphalia."

Superb archers, the Argonauts waited for the hideous creatures to draw closer, and then a desperate battle started. The metal feathers came raining from the sky, but the heroes' arrows sped up like another kind of rain. And while the birds were loosing their feathers at random, not one of the Argonauts' arrows missed its target. The flying monsters fell from the sky in such numbers that the survivors made off to the North, uttering shrieks of terror and despair, and were lost to sight over the horizon.

"We've escaped from the Stymphalian birds," said Jason, "but I see bad weather's setting in. If the sea gets up, it could throw the Argo on the rocks. We must drag her up on shore."

Jason's precautionary measures proved very wise, for that night the sea was not just rough, but mountain-high. The Argo was saved, but in the morning, when the storm had blown itself out, the heroes saw splintered planks floating into shore.

"Some ship was wrecked upon the rocks last night," said Jason. "We must see if there are any survivors." The words were hardly out of his mouth when four bedraggled and exhausted young men appeared from behind the rocks. Who could they be? From their faces they looked very much like Greeks; yet it seemed incredible for any of their fellow-countrymen to be travelling in these distant, unknown parts. Nevertheless, the question was put to them.

"Are you from Greece, friends?"

"We are from Colchis," the young men replied, "and we were on our way to Greece. However, it seems the gods did not intend us to return to the land of our father. We are Aeolians, sons of Phrixus, and as unlucky as he, who suffered so many misfortunes and died in bitterness, far from home."

When Jason heard that these were the sons of his uncle Phrixus, he could not restrain his emotions.

"You are our brothers, then!" he cried, his eyes filling with tears of joy. "I, too, am Aeolian, and the son of Aeson." And he embraced and kissed them one by one.

When they had recovered somewhat from this pleasant surprise and sat down to talk, the Argonauts learned that the four youths had indeed been shipwrecked in the night, and only saved as if by some miracle, when a wave had thrown them on the shore. Then the discussion came round to the topic nearest the Argonauts' hearts. When Jason had explained where they were bound, and why, Cytisorus, one of Phrixus' sons, took up the conversation.

"You have taken on a daunting task," he told them. "I'd say impossible, did I not see such determination in your eyes. The golden fleece is guarded by Aeëtes, son of Helius. Aeëtes, as you must already know, was always a mighty king, but when he acquired the magic fleece his power became invincible – and woe betide the man he learns is plotting, or even thinking, to take the fleece away from him. We know Aeëtes well, for he is our grandfather. Our mother is his daughter Chalciope. His youngest daughter is Medea, a priestess of Hecate and a powerful witch. Aeëtes has a son, too, Apsyrtus, but not by the same mother. He and the girls were brought up by their step-mother. She hated them and they grew to hate her in return, because she only loved her son. In time, Apsyrtus became the king's right-hand man, and a true son of his mother in that he, too, nourished an undying enmity towards his two half-sisters. This bitter dislike extended itself to us. To blacken our names, he told the king we planned to steal the golden fleece. Aeëtes, who would certainly have killed us had we not been his grandchildren and he not feared the anger of the gods, placed us aboard a ship, the vessel which was wrecked last night, and sent us off towards Greece. Baseless fears, however, for he can never lose the golden fleece. A huge dragon, immortal and invincible, guards it unsleeping night and day. And there is something else which makes the golden fleece impossible to steal: the magic powers of Medea, who guards the precious talisman even more jealously than does her father."

"You mean Medea is our most dangerous opponent?" Jason asked Cytisorus.

"She is so skilled a sorceress that she alone could prevent you from achieving your goal," replied Cytisorus, "but Aeëtes wields such power in his hands he has no need of Medea's aid. Nonetheless, he holds her in great esteem, and often has good cause to fear her, for she is the only one who could take this priceless treasure from him if she so wished. She has no call to do this, however. On the contrary, as the king's daughter she has every cause to ensure it is not lost. For all these reasons, and for many others, I tell you that you will never be able to lay your hands upon the golden fleece. So take my advice and return home now. If you as much as set foot in Colchis you may be too late to save yourselves. No one can match the strength and cunning of Aeëtes, no one can disregard a sorceress like Medea, no one can pit himself against such a dragon, and above all, no one can run counter to the wishes of the gods – for it is clearly the desire of the immortals that the golden fleece remain for ever in Colchis. I can see that you are bold and fearless, but it is a shame to throw away your lives."

"We do not return without the golden fleece," said Jason. "And if there are some gods who wish it to remain in Colchis, there are others who would prefer to see it raised upon the altar of Zeus on Mount Laphystium. Our very encounter with you here today is proof that we have powerful gods behind us. Do you think it is mere chance that on this lonely island we have found the only men who could have given us the vital information that we seek – and who will, I trust, afford us any other help we may yet need?"

"We are on your side," the four brothers then said in one voice. And Cytisorus added:

"You have saved us from certain death. We are in duty bound to aid you and risk our lives along with yours."

Shortly afterwards, the Argo was dragged down to the sea and they all set off for Colchis. From then on, with the sons of Phrixus as their guides, the voyage was not difficult. Now they knew exactly where they were going and how they were to get there, which made a great difference.

For nine days they sailed through untroubled waters; but on the morning of the tenth day, the sun was slow to rise. A

... It was Zeus' eagle, going as it did each day to tear open Prometheus' vitals with its beak...

huge mountain blocked its rays.

"The Caucasus!" cried Cytisorus.

Hearing this word, they all thought of Prometheus, the unbowed titan who hung nailed to that towering mass, suffering the most hideous tortures in the world. Just then an eagle flew across the sky, and the heroes' scalps crawled in horror. It was Zeus' torturer, going as it did each day to tear open Prometheus' vitals with its beak. How measureless his love for men must be to bear such horrible torment!

But the melancholy they felt on seeing the great bird of prey turned suddenly to joy when Cytisorus added:

"We have now reached Colchis. Turn to starboard, Ancaeus, and go up towards that estuary. We have come to the mouth of the Phasis, the river which waters the country of Aeëtes."

Soon the Argo had entered the Phasis.

"Heave on the oars," cried Cytisorus, "and pull us up the river! On its bank we shall find Aea, the city of Aeëtes. Our voyage is drawing to its close!"

But after they had rowed against the current for some time, Jason agreed with the sons of Phrixus that it would be better to pull into the side to rest, and go on up the river the next day with their strength renewed.

After they had moored the ship, Cytisorus once more

listed the difficulties which faced them, this time in more detail. However, although they seemed truly insuperable, all the Argonauts, especially Jason, were filled with optimism. And with good cause. For at that very moment, on lofty Olympus, the goddess Hera was seeking a way to obtain effective help for her favourite. This was no easy matter even for a goddess such as she; but Hera had an ally as clear-thinking as all the other Olympians put together: Athena, the goddess of wisdom.

"I must seek Athena's advice," Hera decided. "Her inventive mind and the love she feels for every true hero are certain to be of help to me."

On being told the problem, Athena thought for a while and then replied: "There is one way to prevent the goal the Argonauts have set themselves from remaining an impracticable dream. He must have the only person who could help him on his side. I speak of Medea, the daughter of Aeëtes."

Hera raised her eyebrows in surprise at Athena's suggestion – and not without good reason.

"But how can Medea be made to help Jason, when she watches over the golden fleece even more jealously than her father? Find another solution, Athena, and let's not try to make the impossible come true."

"Many things are possible with a certain arrow, a tiny arrow from the bow of Aphrodite's winged son Eros, which he will shoot into the lovely sorceress' heart. Let us waste no time, but run to find the goddess of love."

"Ah, now I understand!" cried Hera in delight, taking Athena into her arms and kissing her.

Here, then, was the answer to this problem which had seemed so difficult. And it was a very simple answer, as the wisest ones so often are.

When they spoke to the goddess Aphrodite she immediately agreed to help, with obvious pride in the power that she wielded.

"Do not worry," she told them. "It shall happen as you wish. There is no other way that Jason can obtain the golden fleece."

As soon as the two goddesses had left, she called her winged son Eros and commanded him to take his bow and speed to distant Colchis. His mission: to melt Medea's heart towards the hero from Iolcus.

In the meantime, dawn had broken and the Argonauts were preparing to cast off. They were about to bend to the oars when they saw a hawk pursuing a dove through the heavens. A moment later, the dove wheeled sharply, flew above the Argo, then suddenly, seeking protection from the bird of prey, swooped into Jason's enfolding arms. Now the dove was safe, but in its last-minute attempt to strike it down, the hawk flew into the ship's mast so violently that it fell dead on the deck.

"A fair omen," declared Mopsus, the seer from Thessaly. "The dove the bird of love, has found shelter in Jason's arms. Yet another goddess has sent a sign that she is on our side."

Drawing new courage from Mopsus' interpretation of this omen from the heavens, the Argonauts sat cheerfully down at the oars and rowed on up the river, filled with optimism. The sun was low in the West when they caught their first glimpse of Aea, the capital of Colchis. At the city's highest point stood Aeëtes' splendid, gleaming palace. The heroes' hearts began to beat more rapidly. After unimaginable adventures and appalling dangers, they had at last reached journey's end – but how they would obtain the golden fleece, they still had no idea.

Carefully scanning the surrounding countryside, Jason ordered Ancaeus to steer the ship behind a tall stand of reeds where they could not be seen from the city. By now night had fallen, and they still had to decide what they must do next day. Now every man's opinion was of value and Jason called a council of war.

THE GOLDEN FLEECE

Next day, Cytisorus and his brothers led Jason to the palace of Aeëtes. With them was Augeias, another son of Helius, who was anxious to meet this king who was also his brother. At the previous evening's meeting they had come to the conclusion that the best course was for them to present themselves before Aeëtes and tell him boldly that he must give them back the golden fleece. They would tell him they were willing to perform any services he might wish, even at the risk of their lives, providing they received the fleece in exchange. In this way they would make it clear to him that they had not come to snatch it like bandits, but like honest men who deserved to achieve their aim.

What the outcome of this meeting would be, however, none of them could predict. After all, it was bordering on rashness for them to appear before the mighty Aeëtes and tell him they had made a journey of such length with the sole purpose of relieving him of the object he most valued in this world. But then had not the whole mission been a rash one from beginning to end? And would their courage fail them at the very last moment? Not at all. So they boldly set off for the city.

As they approached the gates of Aea, a thick mist enveloped them, sent by Nephele to prevent their being seen by anyone at this dangerous juncture. Cytisorus and his brothers knew the way by heart, of course, and so the whole company reached the palace unobserved, while the mist broke up as soon as they entered the great courtyard.

The court of the king of Colchis now rose up in all its

glory before the admiring eyes of Jason and Augeias. It was said to be the work of the great craftsman Hephaestus who built it to please Helius, the father of Aeëtes. They were especially impressed by a splendidly-carved fountain with four heads, this too the work of the tireless god; but even more impressive than the fountain itself was what flowed from its mouths. Milk gushed from one, wine from another, aromatic oil from a third, while from the fourth ran water which, as Cytisorus explained, poured out hot in winter and in summer cold as crystal. And all these were samples not only of the wealth of Aeëtes, but of the golden fleece's magic powers.

The first to see the new arrivals was Chalciope. With a cry of joy, she ran to embrace the sons she had feared to be lost for ever. But before long the great doors of the palace opened and Aeëtes himself appeared. As soon as he saw Chalciope's sons, and with strangers, too, his face darkened.

"I packed you off to Greece!" he shouted angrily. "Why have you returned?"

"We came back because our ship was wrecked," replied Cytisorus. "We were saved by these fearless men, whom we took for foreigners; they are not foreigners at all, however, but fellow-countrymen of ours from Greece."

"I am your brother, from Elis," announced Augeias, going forward with a smile to embrace him.

But stepping back in an unfriendly fashion, Aeëtes asked them curtly:

"How did you get here? What do you want from me?"

"Jason will explain to you," replied Augeias, pointing out the hero from Iolcus. "He is Phrixus' nephew. As you can see, we have close ties with you."

At that moment, Medea made her entrance. Her great golden eyes, inherited from her grandfather Helius the sun-god, drew Jason and his comrades like a magnet. Medea seemed puzzled to see these strangers with the sons of Phrixus standing in their midst, and she was more puzzled still to hear her father shouting.

"The gods make sure the Symplegades rocks stay closed," he roared, "and Laomedon bars the Hellespont to strangers. What demon brought you here, then?"

Instead of answering, Jason calmly said:

"We salute the mighty king of Colchis, son of Helius..."

As soon as he began to speak, Medea's eyes fixed on this bold stranger, who seemed as handsome as a god. As they did so, Eros, who was lurking behind a column, took aim at her breast and fired his unerring arrow of love.

Nothing more was needed. Suddenly, a man whom she had never seen before became the centre of Medea's world.

One instant was enough to change everything and set her on the road which led to the unknown. But she did not hesitate for a moment; for this foreigner she was ready to give up all. And if he so desired it, she would follow him to the very end of the universe, scorning whatever storms might lie ahead.

Jason noticed Medea, and immediately realised that strange feelings were stirring in the breast of this lovely maiden who stood gazing at him with her great golden eyes. As he spoke to Aeëtes, he sensed that every word he uttered was taking an ever deeper hold on the unknown girl.

"We have made our long and dangerous voyage at the command of Pelias, king of Iolcus," he said. "An oracle has declared that an Aeolian will come to this land in order to take back to Greece a valuable object which once came from there. I am that Aeolian. My name is Jason. I am the son of Aeson, and my orders are to carry off the golden fleece."

"What did you say?" cried Aeëtes in incredulous anger. Medea was no less surprised, but her astonishment only increased the turmoil in her heart.

"I said that I must take the golden fleece and carry it back with me to Greece; and I ask you for it as a friend because you know no man can stand against the will of fate."

"Fool!" cried Aeëtes. "Do you imagine that I will simply

hand over the golden fleece to you? No man will ever tear that precious treasure from me, no matter what oracles or what help he has behind him. Mark this once and for all!"

"And yet you must give it to me," was Jason's calm response. "That ram came from Orchomenus, and its fleece must be returned to Greece. Only then will the soul of Phrixus' father, Athamas, find repose. However, I do not ask you to give it to me with nothing in exchange. I have many comrades with me, and among them are the greatest heroes in all Greece. Give us whatever orders you wish, and we shall be at your command. We can rid your land of bandits and other evil-doers; we can clear your forests of wild beasts and monsters; we can push your enemies back from your frontiers. This, or whatever else you wish, simply command it and it shall be done; all we ask is that you promise us the golden fleece as our reward."

"I need no help from you in any of these matters," growled Aeëtes, "for I have the power to do them on my own. However," he added with a crafty gleam in his eyes, "since you are so eager to risk your life for the golden fleece, there is a task that is worth such a fee. But it is beyond any man's abilities, and when you hear what it is, you will not be so anxious to proceed."

"We have come this far to achieve the impossible,

... “My orders are to carry off the golden fleece.”...

scorning a thousand dangers on our way. Command me and it shall be done. But first swear that you will hand me over the golden fleece in return."

"I swear it, but be warned that it is not victory which awaits you, but defeat; for you must face the insurmountable difficulties which lie before you all alone. Now swear in your turn that you will carry out the task I order."

"I swear by Zeus! I shall succeed, or die in the attempt."

"Then listen to me, since you seek your own destruction: Ares, the god of war, came to me in my sleep and asked me to find a man foolhardy enough to try to plough and sow and reap his rocky field all in one day. I promised Ares that I would sacrifice a hero to satisfy his wishes. Well, now I have found a hero sufficiently in love with death – you are the man!"

"I shall not die!" retorted Jason. "Be sure that I will overcome all obstacles and make you keep your promise."

"Fool that you are," sneered Aeëtes, "do you imagine that I would ever have given you my oath if I believed you could survive the task I set you? Then learn that you will plough Ares' field not with tame and obedient oxen, but with two fire-breathing bulls that were given to me by Hephaestus himself. Approach them and you are doomed. They will charge the instant they set eyes on you, pierce you with their horns and roast you with their flaming breath. And even if you should succeed in taming the beasts and yoking them to the plough, you will then have to till the whole rough and stony field. This you will find an impossible task, for the ploughshare will break the minute it strikes the countless rocks that lie upon the surface of the soil. But let us assume that you do manage to finish the ploughing, then a new danger awaits you when you come to sow – for I shall give you dragons' teeth to scatter in the furrows instead of grains of wheat; and do not wait for green and tender shoots to spring from such a sowing. Huge, savage warriors will burst out from the earth, and you must harvest all of them with your sword before they cut you down. Now go and see if you can do all that – and alone, for those are my conditions. If you succeed, I shall keep my word and let you go to the grove of Ares to take the golden fleece. But don't be in too much of a hurry to congratulate-yourself if you carry out these impossible tasks and reach the grove alive, for there you will face the last and most impossible task of all: how to approach the golden fleece and take it. None of your companions will have the right to go there and assist you, and were you all to go you would be no match for the dragon which guards the place. It is so large that it could hold your whole crew in its belly, and your ship as well. Why, a whole army could not defeat this dragon, for if you do not know already, it is immortal! Don't think that you can catch it in its sleep, either, for this dragon never sleeps. Its eyes are always wide open and alert, searching ceaselessly in every direction and shooting out flames. I have told you all this since you were foolish enough to come here in search of the golden fleece. Now all you have found is certain death; for the road of retreat is no longer open to you; you gave your oath to do whatever I should order!"

"Oath or no oath, I would still take the risk," replied Jason, with a glance at the maiden who regarded him with anxious golden eyes. "I came here for the golden fleece, and without it the way back is closed to me in any case. Tomorrow morning I shall be in Ares' field – without my comrades."

"I see you are a man of spirit," said Aeëtes mockingly. "I shall meet you just one more time, then – and it will give me great pleasure to watch the death of a hero."

"That you can be sure of," retorted Jason bitterly, for he no longer had any hope that he would come out of this alive.

On this note they parted. His hopes in ruins, Jason went back to the Argo with his comrades, while Aeëtes returned to his chambers with a smug look on his face. As for Medea, she went into a corner to weep, miserable and deeply troubled. A tragic dilemma now confronted her. She knew she had invincible magic powers at her command and, if she chose, could help this man to take the golden fleece. But how could she bring herself to do such a thing? How could she betray her father, her own family and the whole of Colchis? On the other hand, how could she refuse help to this stranger for whom her heart now bled? And yet she must leave him to be torn apart by Hephaestus' bulls or cut down by the fearsome giants when they sprang out of the earth, since she had no right to set herself against her father's will. Indeed, one of the first of all the laws the gods laid down was that children should honour and obey their parents. "Oh, great goddess of love!" she cried, "why have you kindled such a flame in my heart? How shall I ever be able to face life again, when though I know I could have saved the man I loved, I let him go to a frightful death!"

Aeëtes' daughter suffered a long agony of indecision, then in the end made up her mind to do a terrible thing. Since she could not defy her father, and her beloved must be left to die, there was no choice but for her to die as well. Searching among the herbs she used to prepare her magic spells, she soon found the plant she needed. A deadly poison could be extracted from its roots. Taking the plant, she kissed it saying, "you will give me the way out."

But at that moment Chalciope rushed in.

"Medea, save us!" she cried. "Your father wants to kill my sons, because they showed Jason the way to Colchis!"

Her eyes streaming with tears, Medea fell into her sister's arms. She told her of the fire which Aphrodite had lit within her breast, explained the terrible quandary she was in, and finally confessed:

"I was about to use this herb to kill myself. You saved me. Now I know what I shall do: I shall overturn our father's plans!" And leaving her sister speechless, she rushed out of the city.

Medea ran for hours across a rugged wilderness until she reached the cliff to which Prometheus hung nailed. At its feet grew a flower, watered by the stoic titan's blood. She broke off a bloom, then hurried to the temple of Hecate, in the forest. Darkness had fallen now, but the moon was full and it was the perfect hour to meet the goddess of the moonlit night. Gazing into the sky and raising high her arms, she called the goddess' name aloud three times. The moon hid itself, and at the same moment Hecate appeared before her, as radiant as the beams which had just faded. The two of them went into the temple together. When they came out a little later, Medea was clutching a small casket to her breast. From the flower which blossomed at Prometheus' feet she and the goddess had prepared an ointment which would give its wearer fearsome and invincible strength. Her heart now light with joy, Medea thanked Hecate and ran off to find Jason.

Meanwhile, gloom reigned aboard the Argo. The more the other heroes tried to persuade Jason not to go to Ares' field but sail for home at once, the more determined he became to stay.

"Your oath doesn't count," Telamon maintained. "It was all a trick to make you put your own head in the noose."

"All that I ask of you, my friends," said Jason in the end, "is that you leave me on my own for a short time."

He felt the need to walk, and wandered off into the woods. He had gone some distance from the ship when he heard a noise beside him. Turning his head, he made out the form of a girl in the darkness.

"Who can you be, wandering alone in the darkness?" he asked in surprise. "Aren't you afraid – unless you are Medea, the daughter of Aeëtes."

The girl came up to him.

"You have guessed rightly. I am she who does not fear the night, but the day that is to come."

"I don't understand what you are saying. There is no hope of my coming out of that ordeal alive. The golden fleece will remain yours for ever. So what reason do you have to be afraid?"

"Till now I have always feared its loss, but now I fear for the one who would take it from us."

"I still don't understand," said Jason. But then he looked into her eyes and there, in the bright moonlight, he saw two tears hanging like shining pearls upon her cheeks. Then Jason understood, and looked at her more closely. She was as lovely as a goddess.

"Listen, Jason," said Medea. "You may find this too hard to believe, but I have come to help you. The gods have given me magic arts, and so I can give you the strength you need to plough the field of Ares and finally help you win the golden fleece as well. Pay close attention to me now, and do as I shall tell you, for we do not have much time. Take this ointment, and when you have first bathed in the river by the light of the moon, anoint your whole body with it. I made it with the aid of the, goddess Hecate, whose priestess I am. It comes from a flower watered by the blood of the titan Prometheus, and that is what gives the ointment all its power. For one whole day you will be stronger than either god or man has ever been before. The bulls' horns

... “I am she who does not fear the night, but the day that is to come.”...

will not be able to pierce your body, nor their fiery breaths burn your skin. Smear your shield with the same magic charm, and it will become so hard that not even the thunderbolts of Zeus will be able to pass through it. Next anoint your sword, and it will even cut through stone. Invincible, and with such power in your hands, you will be able to yoke the bulls and plough up Ares' field. Then you will sow the teeth. They are the same as those that Cadmus sowed at Thebes. Like him, when you see the armed giants sprouting from the earth, take a great boulder and throw it down amongst them. Thinking a war has broken out among themselves, they will start fighting one another to the death. When it is nearly over, throw yourself upon them and use your sword to kill off all the rest. Thus you will emerge victorious from this terrible ordeal. As for the golden fleece, I shall take care of the dragon, and then you will have no difficulty in obtaining it."

"And how shall I repay you for all you have done for me, lovely maiden?"

"Ah, Jason, the goddess of love has lit a burning fire for you within my heart. All I ask of you is love. I want you to take me back with you, make me your wife, raise a beautiful family and live happily with you till the end of our lives. But if ever the day comes when you should cast me out....

"Never!" exclaimed Jason. "I swear this very instant to Hecate, whom you serve, and to the goddess Aphrodite who sent you to save me that I will never turn away the maiden who has abandoned family and home for me, to come to unknown lands and spend her life among strangers."

Weeping with joy, Medea flung herself into Jason's embrace, but a moment later she broke free.

"It is late," she said. "Soon it will be dawn, and you must be ready,before then. Run to do what I have told you, and then go straight away to the field of Ares. Rub the magic ointment on the plough that you'll find there, and then wait for my father. He will come at the rising of the sun. Go now. There is only one thing that you need to know: whatever power lies in the ointment you smear upon your body, your weapons and the plough, you will achieve nothing unless you fight with daring, stubbornness and strength – and I mean your own natural strength; for the greater that is, the more effective will be the power of the charm. I hope that now you understand that everything depends on you – but fear not, I have every confidence in your ability to win. And when night has fallen, come and look for me again in this place."

Jason ran to the river and did as Medea had instructed.

He soon realised that the ointment was indeed miraculous. He felt the blood boiling in his veins, and saw his muscles rippling like steel. A flood of joy and optimism filled him.

In the morning, before the sun had risen, Jason stood waiting in the field of Ares. At this hour there was no-one else in the place. The hero looked around him. It was a rough expanse, its soil all stones and rock. In one corner he saw a stable, no doubt where Aeëtes' bulls were kept. Outside it lay the yoke, and by its side the plough. The hero immediately covered this with ointment, paying special attention to the ploughshare, so it would not break upon the rocks.

A few moments later Aeëtes arrived in his royal chariot. With him were his queen, Eurylyte, his son Apsyrtus and a large following. All had come to see the death of this insolent foreigner who had made his way to Colchis to take away the golden fleece. Medea, who had come with her sister Chalciope, was naturally there for a very different reason. Her eyes quickly met Jason's as he stood there confident and unafraid. Medea, by contrast, was desperately anxious. Would her beloved pass the test, or would he meet a frightful death here on this ugly, rugged hillside that belonged to Ares? For in spite of the strength which her ointment had given him, the feat was still one to daunt the bravest hero. But Chalciope, from whom Medea kept no secrets, gave her sister courage.

"Jason cannot have got as far as this without the assistance of some god," she told her. "Now that he has your help, too, you have nothing more to fear."

Having looked around him and thrown a glance at Jason, Aeëtes raised his hand and gave a signal for the stable door to be opened. Immediately, Hephaestus' bulls came charging forth. Casting a last look at Medea, Jason waited ready for the furious beasts who came thundering out to gore him, with horns lowered and flames shooting from their brazen nostrils. Just as the first bull was about to fall upon him, he seized it by the horns and pinned it to the ground, shaking it to the core. Deftly holding it in front of him as a shield against the second, he forced its head down to the earth. The monster kicked and bucked with its hind legs, but could not free itself. Flames belched from its nostrils, yet these did no harm to the hero, and in the end the bull submitted and allowed him to pass the yoke around its neck. Its partner chose this moment to attack, but very unwisely; for free now of the first, Jason seized this one by the horns as well and forced it to bow its head and be yoked to the other. Then he fixed the yoke onto the plough and leading the now-tamed beasts to the corner of the field, began the ploughing. Goading the bulls on with his sword, he forced them to run up and down the field, dragging the plough, whose share dug deep into the earth, throwing up stones, splitting rocks, uprooting bushes and opening great furrows in the rugged soil. Soon the whole area had been tilled, and the hero ran to Aeëtes with outstretched palm.

"And now the dragons' teeth!" he shouted.

Scarlet with astonishment and rage, Aeëtes handed over the teeth.

"This foreigner is capable of anything," he hissed, "but he won't escape when all those giants fall on him."

As he spoke, Chalciope whispered in Medea's ear:

"He is magnificent! All will be well. You have nothing more to fear."

Jason walked between the furrows scattering the dragons' teeth from his hand. The job was quickly finished and in a few moments gigantic warriors began to spring up from the earth. Soon the whole place was filled with these savage giants, their eyes darting here and there in search of the enemy. From his hiding place behind a bush, Jason seized a huge boulder and hurled it into the middle of the field. A bloody conflict immediately broke out between the warriors, who began to attack one another ferociously. Jason could restrain himself no longer, and lunged into the

... share dug deep into the earth, throwing up stones, splitting rocks, uprooting bushes and opening great furrows in the rugged soil...

fray. The greater number of giants now fell by the hero's hand as he cut them down as tirelessly as if they had been wheat. The sun was sinking into the West when the last of the warriors fell dead. As he toppled to the ground, Jason ran over to Aeëtes to tell him that the harvesting was over – but as soon as the latter saw him coming he mounted his chariot and made straight off for the palace, telling his courtiers:

"I don't want to see that man again unless he's dead! As for the golden fleece, I'm not mad enough to let him try to take it."

But Medea had heard her father, and casting a last admiring look at Jason she took her sister by the hand and ran off with her towards the palace. "None of our father's plans must go unwatched," she said.

Aeëtes stalked into the great hall of the palace beside himself with rage. With a furious glare at those who had accompanied him he shouted:

"Council of war! Immediately!"

"We are all present, sire," announced the most trusted of his generals.

"Tonight we burn the Argo and kill all her crew!"

"I would advise that, too," said Apsyrtus. "But we must hurry if we want to make a thorough job of it."

"Put the army on the alert," commanded Aeëtes. "I will lead the troops myself!"

And then, when all were agreed on action, the plan was ruined by queen Eurylyte, not because she thought it a bad one, but because Hera, who had been following everything, invisible, put these words in her mouth:

"Husband, I agree with what you plan to do, but it may fail unless you calm down first. And if nothing else can calm you, I can!"

With a tender smile she beckoned to him to follow, and Aeëtes, abandoning his council of war, allowed his wife to lead him off to bed.

The generals were relieved at this postponement, and with heavy eyes took themselves off to sleep as well. Apsyrtus, however, was not at all pleased at his mother's intervention. Instead of going to his chamber, he went out and disappeared into the night.

Medea, meanwhile, waited till she heard her father snoring, then ran off to find Jason. She came upon him in the place they had agreed.

"We must go and bring the golden fleece without delay," she told him. "And when we have done so we must leave for Greece immediately. You see, my father plans to burn the Argo and kill you all."

"But is it so quick and easy to obtain?" said Jason in surprise.

"It is impossible – but we shall take it."

"And then?" asked Jason, looking at Medea tenderly.

"And then I shall be with you for ever more, your faithful and devoted partner. But I warn you once again: if.. "

"There will never be an 'if'," protested Jason. "If ever a day comes when I turn you away, I shall merit the harshest punishment. I shall deserve to be abandoned by gods and men alike; to die alone and neglected in the desert and my body eaten by the dogs."

"You do not need to swear such terrible oaths, Jason. I believe you, and that is enough. But now it is time to go to the grove of Ares."

They proceeded by the light of the moon. Suddenly, coming into a clearing, they saw a golden light gleaming from an object which hung in a huge tree. Jason could not believe it: his dazzled eyes were looking on the golden fleece! Near it, however, were two red and glowing circles, just like fire. What could these other strange lights be? Jason did not care to ask. But as they drew closer still, it dawned on him: they were the eyes of the monster, spitting sparks and shooting out flames. Sensing intruders, the dragon suddenly uncurled, opened its cavernous mouth to reveal its terrifying teeth and long, forked tongue, and let out a hideous wail which echoed through the night. Brave and indomitable soul though Jason was, the sense of menace that the dragon radiated was too much for any hero, or even a god, to bear. But while Jason stood rooted in horror, Medea walked on alone, quite undisturbed. Stretching out her hand and uttering magic spells, she soon calmed the great, coiled serpent, and then she called on Sleep, the most willing and invincible of all the gods. Finally, with a leafy branch which she had drenched in a liquid of her own concocting, she sprinkled droplets on the monster's eyelids. Once, twice, three times the spray came down, and then the dragon relaxed, its huge body stretched out across the forest, its head sank to the earth and its eyes closed for the first time since it had been set to guard the golden fleece.

"Quickly, Jason!" Medea cried, "take it down!"

The great moment had come. Jason stepped forward, seized with both hands the precious fleece which glowed beneath the pale light of the moon, and a moment later was hugging it to his breast. It was incredible. He could not believe how fortune had smiled on him so unexpectedly when but a day before all had seemed lost. He gazed into Medea's eyes. Without her help and love one thing was certain: he would be a dead man now. Deeply moved, he stepped forward to embrace her, but Medea pushed him away.

"Run for the ship!" she whispered. "Every second we delay may mean disaster." They had not gone more than a few steps, however, when a shadow loomed from behind a bush, then rapidly disappeared.

"That must have been Apsyrtus," gasped Medea. "He was the only one who did not go to bed tonight. We must get to the ship with all speed, and sail in the night without wasting a moment."

All on board the Argo were keeping anxious watch. Then suddenly they saw Jason come running with Medea. Their anxiety turned to uncontrollable enthusiasm when they saw the hero triumphantly unfold the golden fleece, which shone in golden radiance beneath the rays of the full moon. He hastily helped Medea on board, then jumped on himself and shouted:

"Cast off! Up anchor! All hands to the oars! The golden fleece is ours, but they may catch us any minute. If we don't get away now, we are lost!"

Some of the crew rushed to pull up the anchor, while others loosed the hawsers which held the Argo to the shore – but even as they did so they were casting questioning looks at this stranger Jason had brought with him. He soon satisfied their curiosity:

"This is Medea, the daughter of Aeëtes. The goddess of love herself sent her to our aid. To her magic powers and daring we owe not only the golden fleece, but our salvation. If they chance to catch us, Medea will be the first her father kills. We are bound in duty now to shield her from all danger. But if you owe much to her, I owe everything, and I have sworn to the gods that I will make her my wife and love her all my life."

The Argo had now pushed off and was skimming quickly down the river Phasis. Ancaeus deftly steered her round the bends and through the narrow stretches. Luckily the moon lit up the course ahead, and Lynceus was able to see down to the river bed from far away and warn them of the shoals and rocky patches.

Dawn had not yet broken when the Argonauts made out the broad sea ahead, with the silver light of the setting moon playing on its waves.

"We got away," gasped Jason. "The danger's over now!"

"I do not think so," said Medea. And she was right. For while they had slipped down the river, Apsyrtus had ran panting to the palace and beaten on his father's door fit to break it down.

"Father, get up!" he shouted as the door gave way. "The foreigners have fled with the golden fleece, and Medea is with them. Your daughter has betrayed us, the she-dog!"

"Not only Medea," roared Aeëtes, "but this one here as well, damn her and her caresses!" And with a vicious blow across the face he took his own failure out upon his wife, though certainly not all the fault was hers.

Seething with rage, Aeëtes stormed out of his chamber: "Launch the fleet!" he screamed.

Dawn had hardly broken when the entire fleet of Colchis, with Aeëtes at its head and Apsyrtus as his second-in-command, set off to hunt the Argo down.

"No one must escape!" Aeëtes shouted. "They must all be killed; but make sure that no harm comes to the golden fleece."

"And what about Medea?" asked Apsyrtus.

"Her you will bring to me alive. She merits harsher punishment."

"She deserves to die a thousand times," his son added with bitter malice, little guessing that the hour would come when he would pay for it most dearly.

THE TERRIBLE VOYAGE HOME

With the golden fleece displayed upon her mast, the Argo swiftly drew away from Colchis; but distance brought the heroes no relief – for if one thing was certain, it was that Aeëtes would pursue them.

"There are two ways back to Greece," said Phrixus' son Cytisorus. "One is the route by which you came. The other is via the Danube, a great, broad river we can sail up till we come to another sea which will take us round to the Aegean from the West. This is the way I believe that we should follow. Although it is longer and more tiring, we shall be spared pursuit from Aeëtes, who will never guess that we have headed for the Danube."

They all agreed with Cytisorus, and Ancaeus pulled the tiller round to bring them further northward, where they had heard the Danube flowed into the Black Sea:

The Argonauts sailed quietly on in fair weather for several days until one morning they saw in the distance a long, flat, narrow belt of land which filled the whole horizon to the West. As they drew closer, they saw that thick, tall stands of reeds came right to the water's edge, with what looked like wide bays between them.

"Those are not bays, and it's not sea-water we see between the rushes," said Lynceus. "It must be the Danube, the great river we have been searching for." And soon it became clear that he was right.

Exploring this coastline, they soon found a lush green island where a temple stood out white among the trees.

"Let's put in here," decided Jason. "It is time for us to rest, and an opportunity to thank the gods for keeping Aeëtes off our scent."

They landed on the island and made straight for the temple, which proved to be a small shrine dedicated to Artemis. There the Argonauts made sacrifice to the goddess, begged her to lend them her aid, then returned, feeling calm and comforted, to where the ship lay moored. When darkness came', they lay down on the sand and fell into a deep and unsuspecting sleep. But they awoke at dawn to see the whole sea black with ships. The crafty Aeëtes had guessed which route they would choose, and he had not been wrong. Now the Argonauts were in a desperate situation: there were too few of them to take on so large an enemy force, and it was now too late to slip away unseen.

"Don't give up hope," Medea reassured them. "There is a way for us to save ourselves." And she drew Jason aside.

"Listen," she whispered, "we must deal with Apsyrtus. Without him, that fleet will not know where to turn."

"Yes, but how?"

"There's only one course left to us," came Medea's answer. "We must get him here by trickery. Either that, or we all die today. Now, go to the temple of Artemis and wait, and I will bring Apsyrtus to you there."

And with these words she walked on alone to the island's seaward shore. At that moment, the first and largest vessel of Aeëtes' fleet was just drawing close. Standing in the bows she could see the figure of Apsyrtus, the man who from a brother – different although their mothers may have been – had now become her deadliest enemy. Medea walked forward to the cliff edge. As soon as he set eyes on her, he shouted from the bows:

"You she-devil! I'll catch you and cut you into a thousand pieces! But first you'll watch me kill that foreigner for whom you have betrayed your country, your father and your brother!"

"Oh, Apsyrtus! How could you speak like that?" cried Medea with a wounded air. "And I thought you had come to rescue me from these bandits who stole the golden fleece and dragged me off as well!"

"Liar! I saw you when you went into the grove that night with Jason, to give him the golden fleece!"

"Then did you not see the sword he held and was threatening to plunge into my breast because I would not help him? Are you going to leave me in the hands of these heartless villains, who will slaughter me the moment they see you are attacking, and toss my lifeless body in the sea? Will you let them slay your own sister? I know you do not love me, but will you let your hatred go as far as that? Think carefully, Apsyrtus. Would I ever harm my father, my brother and my homeland? Could I, of all people, ever give away the golden fleece?"

These last words of Medea's were almost drowned in a flood of tears. Apsyrtus was covered in confusion. His sister had been so convincing that now he was ashamed at having spoken so vilely to her.

"But how can I save you if we do not attack?" he asked.

"I told you. If the fleet moves in, they will slay me on the spot. If you want to catch them unawares, come alone to fetch me. Do it now, before they come in search of me. And we must be in time to save the golden fleece, as well. They've got it over there, in the temple of Artemis. Nobody is guarding it because they believe the goddess herself is watching over their loot. But she is on our side. Artemis and Hecate both rule over the moonlit night, and in serving the one, it is as if I also served the other."

Hearing all this, Apsyrtus now trusted his sister so completely that he came over to the island. With Medea at his heels, he ran towards the temple; but there, hidden behind a column, Jason lay in wait for him.

Right on the steps of the shrine, as the unsuspecting Apsyrtus was about to enter, Jason fell on him from behind with his teeth bared in a snarl and his naked sword raised high. His most dangerous enemy, the deadliest threat to his beloved Medea, fell stone dead, staining the white marble of the temple scarlet'.

This murder, however, and the way Medea had deceived her own brother, justly enraged the gods. Zeus was never to forgive either that sword-stroke in the back or her treachery. As for Artemis, the goddess who knew only how to punish, she swore revenge. The defiling of her temple with Apsyrtus' blood was what insulted her most deeply. In vain did Hera try to justify the crime, pleading that it had been committed only to save the Argonauts' lives. Jason and Medea's act was to cost them terrible hardships and perils during their long return to Greece.

But at that moment, Jason did not foresee the fury of the gods. Cheiron's advice: 'fight hard, but never stray from honour' had fled clean out of his mind. All he could see was that thanks to the murder of Apsyrtus the Argo had slipped past Aeëtes, who was searching for the body of his son that he might bury it. The Argonauts, however, had hacked up the corpse and thrown its pieces in the sea to make him lose time searching. Thwarted and inconsolable at the hideous death of his child, he decided to turn back. He did not take all his fleet with. him, however, but only half of it.

"The rest of you," he commanded, "will hunt down Jason and Medea and bring them to me alive or dead. With them you will bring the golden fleece. But if you dare come back with empty hands, I will hang you all in the grove of Ares!"

Before sailing back to Colchis, Aeëtes had to bury the dismembered corpse of Apsyrtus. This was done in a place which from then on bore the name Tomi, which in Greek means 'pieces'. The modern city of Constanza, in Rumania, stands on its site.

Thus the Argonauts were enabled to escape, while the Colchians who remained behind to find them did not know which direction they should take and remained there undecided.

The Argo advanced up the Istrus, as the Danube was called in those days. It was a tiring voyage with the current against them all the way and besides, terrible dangers lurked in these unknown regions. At one of their stopping-places, the fearsome Cynocephali launched an attack upon them. These strange and savage creatures had human bodies and the heads of dogs. They barked ferociously and bit as if they were possessed by devils. A vicious struggle broke out on the shore and even spread on board the ship. Many of the heroes found themselves in desperate straits, and Medea herself let out a cry that made their blood run cold, when one of these monsters reared to spring on her. At the last instant Jason saved her by transfixing the hideous Cynocephalus upon his lance. But the ones who finally saved the Argonauts were the two Boreades, Zetes and Calais, who fought the Cynocephali from the air with

sword in hand. They killed a large number, and so terrified the remainder that they took to their heels with howls of fear.

The Argonauts set off again. Now their passage up the Danube was becoming more and more difficult. For endless days they heaved wearily upon the oars, forcing the ship ever higher. By this time, the Argo was among the mountains, and uncertainty and foreboding began to overtake each of the Argonauts in turn.

"Where are we heading?" many of them asked. "Are we

returning home, or are the gods sending us to our doom among these wild gorges?"

At last, a gap between the hills gave them a glimpse of the broad sea; and on the vast plain which stretched below a great river glinted in the sun. It was on its waters that the Argonauts now placed their hopes.

"That is the Rhône," said Lynceus, "and one of its tributaries has its source near here. We must reach that point."

"But how?" his comrades asked.

There was only one thing to be done. It was almost beyond human powers, but they managed it. Hauling the Argo out of the water, the heroes transported her overland, sometimes staggering along with her on their shoulders, at other times rolling her on tree-trunks they had cut. Up through the wild mountains the Argo was heaved and dragged, and times came when the limp and weary Argonauts were half minded to leave her there and try their luck on foot. But Jason somehow gave them the will to carry on, until they reached the tributary and with a gasp of triumph launched the Argo upon the waters that led down to the Rhône.

They now sped south towards the mouth of that great river, their strong strokes aided by the swift flow of its current. The very next day they reached the coast. Before them lay the mighty Western Sea, which would lead them back to Greece. Their terrible ordeal was drawing to a close. With a light heart, Orpheus took up his lyre and soon the rousing song on all their lips echoed like a paean of victory upon the boundless azure of its depths. In this cheerful mood, the Argonauts paid no attention to the darkening sky, nor did they notice that the wind was getting up and bringing high seas with it. But their song was cut off in mid-note when a blinding fork of lightning split the ship's mast in two and set fire to the sail. The wrath of Zeus had descended on them in all its fury. The god who rules the clouds and grasps the thunderbolts in his strong hands could no longer tolerate the spectacle of the Argonauts returning gaily homeward as if they had nothing on their conscience, and the murder of Apsyrtus had never been committed. At the mercy of Zeus' anger, the Argo tossed like a cork on the ever-swelling waves. Clinging to the broken mast, Jason bellowed out a stream of orders that would enable them to ride the storm. With splendid courage, the Argonauts held the ship against the wind to prevent seas smashing from the side and overturning her. Only Zetes and Calais, whose actions had so often saved the crew in previous crises, now paid no heed to their captain's orders, but glared in silent hatred at Medea as she clung in terror to Jason's legs. Finally Zetes could restrain himself no longer.

"It's her fault the gods have sent this storm to lash us!" he cried out. "No voyage was ever lucky with a sorceress on board."

"The blood of Apsyrtus pursues us still," added Calais. "If we want the seas to drop, there's only one solution: throw Medea to the waves!"

"You're mad, the pair of you!" roared Jason.

And Euphemus, the most kind-hearted of the Argonauts, agreed.

"Thanks to Medea, we all escaped from death. Can we sacrifice her now to save our own skins? Do that, and the gods will drown us all the sooner."

"You could all be lost if Jason and Medea are not absolved of the murder of Apsyrtus," came another voice.

They all looked round wide-eyed, for this was not a human voice that they were hearing. It came from the wooden figurehead of Hera, whose lips they could even now see opening and closing.

"On the first island you will come to," went on the goddess, "lives the sorceress Circe, daughter of Helius and thus the aunt of both Medea and Apsyrtus. It is from her that you must seek forgiveness. If she grants it, you will return to Greece; if not, then never hope to see your homes again, for the Furies will pursue you for all time."

Once the wooden head had ceased to speak, some unknown power drove the Argo onwards through the gale, cleaving the white-topped waves until she gently came to rest upon the sands of a deserted shore; and as she did so, the storm died inexplicably away. The Argonauts looked in bewilderment at this unknown place, which seemed to be an island. Then, on its summit, they made out a castle. Now they were sure: they had somehow come to rest on the isle which Circe ruled. The goddess Hera had helped them yet again – but what would happen next?

Jason and Medea, two of Phrixus' sons and another three Argonauts took the road which led up to the castle. As they drew closer, they saw it was a gleaming palace which lay before them. Leaving the others, Jason and Medea proceeded into the great hall alone. There, on a tall and gilded throne sat Circe, lovely as a goddess. And in her eyes there shone that golden light which proved beyond all doubt she was a daughter of Helius, the Sun. Her guards were not men, but two lions, sprawled before her on the dais. As soon as the strangers entered, the beasts sprang up with threatening growls, displaying rows of pointed teeth. But Circe reassured the lions with a gesture and invited her visitors to approach.

Jason spoke, and having told her who he was, related his whole troubled story from the start. Yet while he recounted everything that had befallen them, and in full detail, he avoided giving any other name away besides his own. However, seeing that Circe was listening to him with an air that was hostile rather than sympathetic, he added:

"I have told you all this so you may see we had no other way to save ourselves. If we resorted to deception, crime and the defiling of the temple, it was not to save our own lives merely, but those of all our comrades too. But now the Furies are pursuing us; and that is why we have come here to beg you to show mercy, and cleanse us of this sin."

"You ask forgiveness and absolution for a deed as foul as this without even telling me your victim's name?"

In a voice that was hardly more than a whisper, Jason confessed:

"We murdered Apsyrtus, the son of king Aeëtes.

"Whom did you kill?" cried Circe, rising from her throne. "Apsyrtus? and in a temple, too?"

And while her cry of accusation still rang out, Circe's face began to crack with wrinkles, her hair grew white and sparse, her nose drew down into a thin, pinched hook, her hands grew parchment-like and bony, and her fine robe became a black and melancholy shroud.

"And you came to me?" she hissed, her voice now shrill and quavering. "You came to Aeëtes' sister to be cleansed of your foul crime? Where did you find the insolence?"

Jason was struck speechless by Circe's sudden transformation and the harsh reproach which followed; but now Medea took up the pleading.

"It would never have happened if Apsyrtus had not come in pursuit of us, seeking our deaths," she explained.

But Circe was paying more attention to Medea's eyes than to her words; for in them shone that same gold light that glowed in hers.

"But you are Medea!" she cried. "How did you get involved in such a hideous murder?"

"Yes, I am Medea – whom Apsyrtus hated though I'd never done him any ill. And if I left my country for those strangers, and gave my aid to Jason, it is because Aphrodite lit the fires of passion in my heart, and made me yearn for this man's love more deeply than I ever loved my father, or even my mother, whom I lost when I was young and helpless."

Circe was softened by Medea's plea, but even so she added:

"Yet Apsyrtus was still your brother, even though different women bore you."

"Yes, a woman who taught him to hate me and my sister," Medea said to justify herself.

"It is a terrible thing for brothers and sisters to hate one another, said Circe sternly. "To sink to killing is more frightful still."

But even as she spoke her withered face bloomed into smoothness once again, her hair grew dark and lustrous, and soon the mighty sorceress was once more the young and lovely woman she had been before.

Jason and Medea looked on in awe as the beauty flooded back into her face.

"Do not wonder at the change," said Circe. "The gods have blessed me with the wisdom which accompanies old age, together with the tender freshness of first youth. I am no longer angry with you. Come with me now and I shall cleanse you of your crime." And with these words she took them by the hand and led them to a spring.

There she slaughtered a young lamb, and with its blood she washed their hands. Then she commanded them to bathe in the waters of the spring, and afterwards she told them:

"What you begged of me is done. Only the gods know why, but I have taken a liking to you both. Perhaps because you, Jason, were ready to risk your very life to bring the golden fleece back to your homeland; and you, Medea, because you gave up all for love. But a crime is a crime, and now I, too, am tainted with your guilt. I have betrayed my brother Aeëtes, and as a seer I know the day will come when I shall pay for it. It does not matter; I have done what I think best. And now pay careful heed to me. Once cleansed, no mortal has the right to charge you; the gods, however, judge in different ways. They are beholden to no-

... soon the mighty sorceress was once more the young and lovely woman she had been before...

one but themselves. The goddess Artemis will never offer you forgiveness for the defiling of her temple, and you will pay for it with countless sorrows and misfortunes before you finally return to Greece. Your lives will be hard and storm-tossed to the end. I grieve to warn you of so many evils yet to come – but I would not wish it to be said that Circe could not foresee the future clearly."

For all this, Jason and Medea left the great sorceress feeling as if a leaden weight had been lifted from them. So great was their relief at absolution that there was no room in their hearts for sadness at Circe's gloomy predictions of what lay before them.

Next morning, the Argo set sail once more. The weather was fair, and all the crew now reassured and confident. Then, as they cleaved the clear blue waters, the meltingly sweet sound of women's voices reached them from afar. The Argonauts were enchanted by their song, innocent of the evil it concealed; for, alas, they were approaching the island of the Sirens. At first sight, these were ravishingly lovely creatures as they glided on their sleek white wings, but their legs were those of birds of prey, with murderous, slashing talons. Worst of all, they lived on human flesh alone. All voyagers who ventured near the Sirens' lair became their unhappy victims, whether or not they had intended to set foot on the island. For the Sirens sang so sweetly that they literally bewitched all who sailed by; and even when the sailors knew what fate awaited them, they could not resist the urge to rush ashore. The same fate was about to befall the Argonauts who, on hearing the call of those enticing voices, forgot all that they had ever been told about the creatures and bent to their oars to arrive with all speed possible at this island of death.

Fortunately there was one among them whose ears the Sirens were not able to seduce. It was Orpheus who, seeing the mortal danger they were rushing into, took up his lyre and immediately began to sing. His voice rang out and drowned the sweet song of the Sirens; and just in time the Argonauts came to their senses, realised the peril they were in and changed course to evade the witches' deadly call. Only one of them could not resist. This was the handsome Butes, who dived entranced into the sea to hasten to their side. But the goddess Aphrodite could not bear to see his good looks torn by those cruel claws, and rushed to save him. Taking him up in her arms, she carried him off to Sicily; and there, though the young man was inconsolable at first, she succeeded in erasing all trace of the Sirens from his memory with her own matchless charms. It is even said that Eryx, who later ruled in that great island, was the fruit of the love which Aphrodite lavished on the handsome Butes.

But now the Argonauts sailed on from danger into danger.

All unsuspecting, they found themselves a few days later before the straits of Scylla and Charybdis. This was a narrow channel which seemed innocent enough, but was the lair of two hideous monsters – one upon each bank. Voyagers who did not know what perils lay concealed there and tried to sail between them were never seen again. Only a few shattered timbers from their ships would reveal the fate that had befallen them.

Scylla was a huge dragon with a writhing mass of snake-like necks topped by great dogs' heads with mouths yawning so wide they could swallow a whole man in a single gulp. Charybdis was another terrible dragon who could suck in waves so fast, and in such quantities, that the rocks and sand of the sea bottom were laid bare. Entire vessels were engulfed like this. Even more awe-inspiring was the moment when the monster blew out the water it had sucked into its maw. Then the sea boiled so wildly that the foam and spray rose up like clouds, while masts, planks, oars and other wreckage of the ships it had devoured were tossed into the heavens. But no men ever found their way out of its hungry belly.

No crew had ever yet sailed up the strait between Scylla and Charybdis and lived to tell the tale – and neither would the Argonauts, who were now approaching the narrows without sensing any need for caution. But Hera, who kept ceaseless watch over the Argo, ran to warn the sea-goddess Thetis. She was the only deity who had ever married a mortal – and he was now on board the ship that was sailing to its doom. Peleus was his name, and by sheer determination this hero had once defeated the goddess in a wrestling match where the odds were all against him, thus winning her admiration and her love. As soon as Thetis learned that her husband and his comrades were in deadly peril she immediately sought the aid of her sisters the Nereids. Swimming like dolphins round the Argo, the fifty daughters of old Nereus kept Scylla and Charybdis cowering at bay. The heroes were through the narrows before the hideous monsters could find the courage to attack – but the many heads of Scylla growled so menacingly, and so terrifying was Charybdis' hissing wail of greed, that had it not been the heroic Argonauts that were making the passage, but some other voyagers, they would certainly have been driven mad by fear.

The gauntlet had been run, but now they were driven across the sea for days on end, without a sight of land. The wind was so unsteady that it blew them first towards the West, then eastwards once again. Whenever Lynceus made out a distant coast ahead, the wind would turn and blow them out to sea. As their supplies of food and water dwindled, their plight grew steadily more desperate. Yet now it was the turn of the goddess Hera to show her concern for them once more. She hastened in search of Aeolus, king of the winds, and commanded him to send Zephyrus, the gentle western breeze, to lead the Argo to the nearest shore. Aeolus obeyed the mighty goddess, and Zephyrus brought the vessel to the friendly harbour of the Phaeacians, on the island that is known today as Corfu.

The Argonauts were welcomed by king Alcinous himself. He immediately gave orders for the royal table to be spread in honour of the new arrivals; and when he learned that his guests had such an heroic achievement to their credit he was so carried away by his enthusiasm that he invited them all to stay in the royal palace for as many days as they required to rest and build their strength up. They had hardly sat down to eat, however, when from the open windows of the palace they saw foreign ships entering the harbour. Anxious, they went down to the quay at once to see if the newcomers were friends or enemies. As soon as the Argonauts set eyes on them, their hearts sank. The ships were Colchian, part of the force that Aeëtes had left behind at the mouth of the Danube, with orders to bring Jason and Medea back to him, dead or in chains.

The Colchians disembarked peacefully enough; but as soon as they spotted the Argonauts they let out a piercing war cry and unsheathed their swords. Faced by this danger, the Argonauts drew their weapons, too. However, before they could come to blows, Alcinous stepped between them.

"Listen!" he cried. "We are more than ready to welcome all our foreign guests – but we do not permit them to threaten anyone with naked swords. If you persist in fighting among yourselves, I have an army large and strong enough not only to prevent it, but to round up and punish the ringleaders. So put your swords back in their sheaths, starting with you who drew them first. Then let the leaders of you new arrivals come up to the palace to eat and drink, as did the Argonauts, and tell me the reason you were about to start a fight. If I find your cause was justified, I shall see to it that you receive satisfaction without any bloodshed."

And so the leaders of the Colchians went up to the palace and, having told Alcinous who they were and why they had been combing the seas, finally said:

"We would ask you to hand us over all the Argonauts in chains – but since they are your guests, we know you won't do this for us; but we do at least request you to make them give us back the golden fleece, because it is ours and they stole it from us; and Medea, because she is the daughter of our king, Aeëtes. For as you well know, stolen goods must be returned to those that lost them, and daughters to their fathers."

Alcinous gave careful thought to the Colchians' demands, but finally decided:

"I cannot oblige the Argonauts to return the golden fleece to you, for it is theirs by right. I know the whole story: Aeëtes himself promised the pelt to Jason if he could plough, sow and harvest Ares' field. In this matter your demands are unjustified, and I will not put myself in the wrong by supporting you. As for Medea, you are right in saying that daughters are their fathers' property – but you should not forget that wives also belong to their husbands. For this reason, before I hand Medea over to you I must first ascertain whether she is Jason's wife: and I am afraid that if she is, she will have to remain with her husband."

Alcinous then asked his wife Arete whether she knew if

Jason and Medea were married.

"I do not know," she answered, "but I shall find out and let you have the answer."

In fact, Arete already knew that the couple were not yet wed, but anxious to help, she ran to warn them both.

"There is only one solution," she said. "You must be married at once." They both accepted without hesitation. True, Jason had imagined his wedding very differently. He had dreamed of an imposing ceremony in the palace at Iolcus in which he would be crowned king, and at the same moment Medea would become both his wife and queen. He had often thought of the great joy this would give not only to his aged parents, but to all his fellow-countrymen, since this marriage would also free them from the yoke of Pelias' tyranny.

But even though the wedding was now destined to take place in hasty secrecy, it would not be lacking in ceremony and grandeur. Arete asked Macris, a forest nymph, to allow the marriage rites to be celebrated in her cave, which she willingly agreed to. It was like a treasure cave out of some fairy tale, with crystal walls and a ceiling of many-coloured stalactites. The other nymphs of the island came to lend their help as well, spreading the bridal bed in a small cave to one side, then strewing it with sweet-scented rose-petals.

Queen Arete herself, with Macris at her side, washed, combed and decked the bride in white, then led her out to stand at Jason's side. To all who saw them, he and Medea seemed as radiant as a god and goddess newly descended from Olympus, for Aphrodite herself had bestowed some of her own beauty on the bride and groom that day. All the Argonauts were present, while the nymphs formed a circle round the couple, their breasts garlanded with flowers of many colours. To the sweet strains of Orpheus' lyre, the guests showered grains of wheat upon the happy couple and serenaded them with songs of joy and love.

As soon as the marriage had been celebrated, Arete hastened back to her husband.

"Jason and Medea were married just a short while ago," she told him.

"I am glad to hear it," Alcinous replied. "I have taken a liking to those two young people, and I would not like to see their happiness destroyed."

So the Colchians were unable to lay their hands either on the golden fleece or on Medea. Knowing what fate would await them if they returned empty-handed to their country, they never went back home. Some stayed on the island of the Phaeacians and entered into the service of Alcinous, while the remainder, angry because that monarch had not

... To all who saw them, he and Medea seemed as radiant as a god and goddess newly descended from Olympus...

bowed to their demands, went elsewhere to seek their fortunes, finally casting anchor among some islands off the Dalmatian coast which have been called the Apsyrtides ever since.

Whatever the feelings of the Colchians, the Argonauts were delighted with the outcome, and after thanking Alcinous for the rich gifts and provisions he had showered on them, they went on board the Argo and sailed out of the harbour.

Now they were in familiar waters, and the happy oarsmen pulled away with a will. In a matter of days they would reach Iolcus with the golden fleece and their long and terrible ordeal would at last come to an end.

Now driven forward by her oars, now helped along by the wind, the Argo made steadily for the home port she had left so long before. She soon reached the southern shores of Greece, then, having rounded the Peloponnese, skirted the coast of Attica and from there continued northward until at last she entered the gulf of Iolcus. It seemed that Zeus had forgiven Jason and Medea and the wrath of Artemis had cooled at last.

But had it? Alas, no. The gods were playing the cruellest of games with them. They intentionally let the Argo draw in close, so that the Argonauts could make out the houses of Iolcus from afar; and then, just when all hearts were beating fast in expectation, and Jason was pointing out to Medea the smoke which rose up from his father's chimney, all the fury of the elements broke suddenly upon them. A terrifying whirlwind ripped the sail in two and snapped the mast, a great wave smashed both tillers and then a fierce gale from the shore seized on the Argo, swept her before it from the gulf and carried her far away into the broad sea. With Zeus to back her, Artemis was now taking her pitiless revenge.

Nine days the Argo fled before the storm-tossed waves, until at last she found herself upon the coast of Africa. Only when she had been driven high and dry upon the Libyan sands did the winds consent to drop. Weary to the bone and bitterly deceived, the heroes staggered onto this unwelcoming and barren coast, while Iolcus once more faded into a distant, long-desired but elusive dream. Even so, to be thrown on any shore was a relief after a buffeting such as the heroes had received; and since night had fallen, their knees were weak and their eyes drooping with fatigue, they all collapsed upon the sand and sank into a deep sleep.

In the morning they were awakened by the scorching

rays of the sun. Early though it was, the heat was already oven-like. They looked around them and their hearts sank. Nothing but endless sand-dunes met their eyes in every direction. Not a blade of green grass was to be seen, not even a dried-up plant to show that once some rain had fallen here.

The Argonauts were plunged into utter despair. Only Jason kept his spirits high.

"Listen, brothers," he said. "We have come through many trials, and this is just another. If we allow despair to take its hold on us, then we shall leave our bones here in the desert. Our only hope is if we fight to stay alive. And we know how to fight! Our first task now is to drag the Argo well above the water-line, then sew her sail up, step the mast and make good all the other damage she has suffered. But everything must be completed by this evening – if we stay here any longer we shall die of thirst."

Jason's words gave the heroes the will to fight again. Now confident they would survive this new ordeal like all the others, they pulled the Argo up on shore and set to work regardless of the burning sun and the sand which scorched their bare feet.

By nightfall everything was ready.

"Tomorrow we must launch the ship and leave," said

Jason. But Medea disagreed:

"We cannot sail unless the gods first give a sign that they will not block our way once more. Till now, we have been counting on our luck alone – and look where it has led us."

"You are right," replied Jason, "but how shall we know?"

"We shall find a way if we try."

And so, while all the other Argonauts were asleep, Jason and Medea went searching in the desert. As they wandered, they heard the sound of women's voices coming from the direction of the sea. Before them stood a low sand dune. Climbing to its summit, they saw beneath them in the moonlight three maidens clad in white who were dancing and singing on the seashore.

"Where did these women spring from in the middle of the desert?" Jason wondered.

"They must be the daughters of Libya," Medea said. "They are nymphs of the wilderness, and are wise in many matters." And with these words she ran boldly down to them. Jason followed, but more hesitantly.

As the nymphs caught sight of them they stopped their dance, and when Medea and then Jason had drawn close, one of the three asked:

"Is that your ship lying on the sand?"

"Yes, it is ours," Medea replied. "A terrible storm cast us up on this coast."

"Then you must have drawn the fury of some goddess on you by insulting her," the maiden observed.

"If you know that," went on Medea, "then perhaps you can tell us how we can escape from this place."

"Yes," came the answer. "We know and we shall tell you. You must wait until you see the sea-goddess Amphitrite unharness her white horses, and only then can you resume your voyage. But, mind you, only thus: you will do for your ship what the ship has done for you till now. You will proceed in this manner until you reach the end of the world – and I warn you that your road will be a hard and weary one. But in following it you will placate the goddess whom you have offended and finally be enabled to sail for your home port."

And with these words the three nymphs linked hands once more and danced off into the night, their song fading into the distance.

Jason and Medea stared at each other in amazement, then ran to wake their comrades. But no-one could explain the strange message they had been given. Nevertheless, they spent the whole night gazing at the sea in case they saw Amphitrite taking the bridles off her horses.

"We are wasting our time," said Ancaeus. "Nobody has ever set eyes on the wife of earth-shaker Poseidon – so how likely are we to see her, and with horses too? And what horses, besides? Does Amphitrite have such steeds? Then what does it mean: 'Do for the Argo what she has done for us till now'? Don't tell me we've got to carry her on our shoulders, just as she has carried. us so long? It's all nonsense, I tell you."

The words were hardly out of his mouth when, from a foaming wave which broke upon the sand, there galloped two white stallions.

"You see, the nymphs were right," Medea smiled. "Amphitrite has set her chariot-horses free to graze!"

"But what shall we do now?" asked Jason. "Surely not set off for the end of the world with the Argo on our shoulders, like Ancaeus said?"

"That is exactly what we must do," replied Mopsus. "Only by driving us to the limits of our endurance will the goddess Artemis be placated."

The heroes steeled themselves for the ordeal. With a mighty heave of their strong arms, they pulled the Argo free and hoisted her upon their shoulders. Now a terrible forced march began. The heroes' feet sank deep into the burning sand. Sweat streamed from their bodies as they struggled on. The sun beat down remorselessly upon their wind-flayed bodies. But they pressed forward. Six hideous days they staggered on like this – and worst of all the sea lay always at their side, calm and mocking.

"Let's launch the Argo in the water," the Boreades protested. "What we are doing is sheer folly."

"It is the will of the gods that we carry her upon our shoulders," Jason replied.

"To the end of the world?" the Boreades retorted.

Jason did not like what he heard.

"We are all suffering," he snapped, "but I see that you are the only ones to complain."

Shamed by his words, Zetes and Calais fell silent.

The next day, their water came to an end. Now it was a hundred times worse for the heroes, but they lurched grimly on. Medea, however, could stand the pace no longer, and sank down on the sand. Jason left the Argo and ran to lift her to her feet.

"Go on alone," she gasped. "This is journey's end for me."

Jason took her in his arms; and when Medea had recovered somewhat he left her to walk on and put his shoulder to the Argo's keel once more. When she sank into the sand

... Jason left the Argo and ran to lift her to her feet...

again, he left the Argo and went back to help her, and this went on all day.

By the next morning, what little food was left had been consumed.

Hunger, thirst and exhaustion were taking their relentless toll upon the heroes.

Medea toppled headlong in the sand, as lifeless as a corpse.

"Let's leave the sorceress and go on," the Boreades growled once more. "She's to blame for everything!"

Kind-hearted Euphemus was spurred to anger by their words:

"Why don't you two just leave us to our fate?" he cried. "After all you're the only ones with wings."

The Boreades sank their heads in shame. They loathed Medea, it was true; but betray their comrades? No, that they could never do. And so the long-drawn torture of their march continued, with Jason carrying Medea in his arms. Another day of terrible suffering went by; and next morning they set off once again. As the sun rose high, and the heat grew past all enduring, Jason swayed, then fell face forward in the sand with Medea. He alone had borne his burden without respite, and now his powers were at an end.

"Go on alone, my friends," he gasped. "We shall stay

here. It is the will of the gods."

The Boreades looked down at Medea with hatred. They were about to speak, when Euphemus stepped in front of them.

"Be silent!" he commanded.

And then, having helped Jason to his feet, he lifted Medea onto his shoulders, crying: "Forward, comrades!"

Another, even more terrible day dragged by. In the evening, they sank down on the sand, half dead from exhaustion, thirst and hunger. The sun rose on the eleventh day of their journey into hell. They staggered to their feet, but felt as weary as though they had been shouldering their burden the whole night long. They did not get very far. As soon as the sun began to burn with all its force, they dropped down on their knees and let the Argo topple on its side.

"We can go no further," many of them gasped. And not a voice was raised in disagreement.

A long time went by, yet no-one spoke of lifting up the Argo once again. Worst of all, they were now far from the sea – but had the sea been near, and had the gods raised no gales and storms against them, would they still have had the strength to fight off hunger and thirst until they reached a harbour beyond this desert? All hope was lost, it seemed. Around them stretched the sands, boundless and bare, and above them rose the scorching sun in a sky of perfect blue whose beauty had never before seemed so hostile to the parched and weary heroes.

The sun sank down into the West and the Argonauts still lay stretched out on the sand, each one praying for a speedy death to put an end to his sufferings. Then, suddenly, Lynceus cried out:

"Look at the sun!"

"What do you see?" asked Jason, hope lighting up his face.

"Look at the sun!" Lynceus cried out once more. And as he did so, the heroes all struggled to their knees and gazed westwards.

But they could see nothing except the sun sinking behind a mountain.

"All I can see," said Jason finally, "is a tiny mark on the sun's disc, a little black spot on the mountain's peak."

"But a little spot which tells us we are saved!" cried Lynceus. "What your eyes see as a mere nothing, mine make out as Atlas, bearing the arch of the heavens upon his shoulders. Courage, brothers! We have reached the end of the world!"

Where did those half-dead heroes find the strength to let out such cries of joy from their dry throats? Where did they find the strength to spring straight to their feet and take the Argo in their hands? And where did they find the strength to march all night towards the spot where they had seen that tiny speck silhouetted against the setting sun? And yet they found it. Hope gave them wings, and the sure faith that all their frightful tortures were drawing to a close.

When the twelfth day dawned their enthusiasm knew no bounds. In the distance Atlas, the unresting titan, loomed huge, while before them lay a lush green garden filled with trees of all varieties, their branches heavy with fruit. The crystal sounds of water in a nearby river fell on their ears like heavenly music, while at their side the blue sea stretched once more. Letting the Argo slip from their shoulders, the heroes rushed to the river, threw themselves face forward on its bank, thrust their heads into its waters and drank and drank and drank. Only Jason held back for a moment. First he took water in his cupped hands and sprinkled it on Medea's face; then, going back for more, he gave it her to drink. Only when Medea's thirst was slaked did he plunge his head into the river like the others.

The long torture of their thirst was over.

Now they needed food – and at that moment three maidens came out from the garden bearing great baskets filled with ripe and luscious fruit.

"Come and eat," they told the heroes and set the overflowing baskets down before their greedy eyes, while one of them ran to offer Medea the first and choicest of the fruit.

Rescue had come to the Argonauts when all hope seemed lost. Soon they felt new life surging through their veins and their exhaustion fell from them like heavy weights. Medea, too, was well and strong again. Yet they were puzzled. The maidens seemed to have been expecting them, so who could they be? But their bewilderment did not last long. Medea had recognised the three.

"You are the Hesperides," she said. "It was you, I have been told, brought up the goddess Hera when her mother carried her to this place as a small child."

"Yes," they replied. "We are the daughters of Hesperus, and the goddess Hera is our dearest friend. It was from her we learned you would be coming here."

The Argonauts were touched by this: while all the other gods were putting them through torments, Hera had still continued giving them her aid and showing them that she was on their side.

But more moving and impressive still was their meeting with Atlas, the mightiest of all the gods in bodily strength. Having fought and lost against Zeus in the Battle of the

Titans, he was punished by being made to bear the great arc of the heavens upon his shoulders for all eternity. It was a back-breaking ordeal, and one from which he could never free himself for if he relaxed his hold upon the crushing burden the sky would crash down on the earth and he and all the world be crushed. Secure in this knowledge Zeus ruled over gods and men with an untroubled mind.

If the Argonauts felt sympathy and admiration for the mighty titan, Atlas felt no less for them.

"Nobody comes to the end of the world," he said, "so how did you reach here – and carrying a whole ship on your shoulders, too? But why do I ask," he continued, "since I know the answer: you are men born to struggle – and to struggle on united, that is all. Yet you will find it is no easy task to leave this place. If you are to regain the open sea, it can only be by the will of Triton. Of all the gods, he alone can help those who are lost in unknown waters."

But the heroes were now confident that all would go well, and the next day, they gaily launched their ship into the waves and set off once again.

They turned the bow towards the rising sun, for now that they had come to the furthest reaches of the West, their only homeward course lay to the East. However, they had not sailed far when they saw a coastline barred their way. All they could do was alter course and head North, in the hope that they would find some channel through. Not only did they not find such an exit, but they were obliged to keep bringing the Argo's head round in the direction of the setting sun until they found, after a long and tiring journey, that they had come full circle and were back where they had started. It was now clear to all of them that they were not on the open sea, but trapped in some huge lake.

"How can we escape from here?" asked Ancaeus. "Let's hope we do not have to heave the Argo on our shoulders once again and set off through the burning desert!"

Then Jason remembered Atlas' words.

"We must ask the sea-god Triton for his help," he said.

"But first we must make sacrifice to him," Telamon remarked, "and we have no animal to offer."

"However, we have the finest hunter in all Greece – the one who killed the Calydonian Boar," said Peleus, pointing out Meleager.

Meleager jumped eagerly to his feet.

"Let's go together, Peleus!" he cried. "To tell the truth, I don't know which of us is the better hunter."

It did not take the two friends long to bring back a live

deer. An altar was immediately built and the beast sacrificed to Triton while they prayed that he would lead them to the open sea.

The prayers had scarcely left their lips when they heard a trumpet sounding.

It was Triton himself approaching, cleaving the waters and blowing on a conch-shell. Moments later, he stood amongst them.

In appearance he was less like a god than an ordinary young man, burnt a deep brown by the sun as are all seafaring folk. In one hand he held his horn, and in the other a ball of earth. Casting a searching eye over the Argonauts he picked out Euphemus, went up to him, and handed him the lump of clay he had been holding.

"This is for you," he said, "and you deserve it."

All the Argonauts looked on in surprise. What was the value of a clod of soil? Yet Euphemus received his gift with joy. What did it matter that it was a mere piece of earth, when it had been presented to him by a god?

"Now, all of you, get into the ship and follow me," said Triton.

They climbed on board the Argo, sat down at the oars and rowed off. Before them went the god, who was now no longer wholly human but a dolphin from the waist downwards, with a great, sickle-shaped tail. If Triton could transform himself in this amazing way, the Argonauts had no doubt that he would also be able to guide them out of the lake. But when they saw him swimming full speed for the shore, their faces dropped. If they followed as he had instructed, the Argo would end up on dry land! Nervously, the Argonauts dug in their oars and stopped the vessel's forward motion, but Triton beckoned them to keep on moving. And then they saw that this was exactly what they must do – for a miracle was taking place before their eyes: as the god moved onwards, so the land before him sank beneath the waves and a channel opened up ahead of them. And thus the Argo sailed on with dry land on either side until she finally reached the broad and open sea. There Triton halted, wished them a fair voyage, then swam back into the canal – and as he returned towards the lake, the land closed in on either side of him once more. These landlocked waters were said to be the sea-god's kingdom, and for that reason the lake is still called Tritonis.

Their hearts warm with gratitude for the god who had saved them, the Argonauts set sail for the East. Now all the elements were on their side and a fair wind drove the Argo swiftly towards Greece. After their terrible ordeal in the

... They climbed on board the Argo, sat down at the oars and rowed off...

burning desert it seemed beyond belief that no obstacles lay in their way as they sailed on for the homeland they all so longed to see.

Within a few days they caught sight of land. With enthusiastic shouts they gazed at the high mountains which now rose above the horizon. They were the familiar peaks of Crete. Only two or three days now, and they would reach Iolcus; but their water supplies were running low and so they decided to make a brief stop. They had sailed in close to the shore, looking for a sheltered anchorage, when suddenly a huge boulder crashed into the water at the Argo's side and nearly sank her. Had it fallen on the ship, she would have been smashed to matchwood. The heroes looked up into the mountains and saw a giant, the colour of bronze, in the very act of hurling another great rock down on them. Ancaeus just had time to pull the tiller over before the missile could do the Argo any harm.

"Why are you throwing rocks at us?" the Argonauts shouted. "We are not pirates. In the name of Zeus, the god of hospitality, all we ask is a little water – nothing more."

"That creature knows nothing of Zeus, nor of hospitality," remarked Medea. "He is Talos, the bronze giant, guardian of Crete. He never sleeps, but ceaselessly patrols the island's coasts – and woe betide any foreign ship that dares approach its shores. He cares not whether there are pirates or peaceful voyagers on board. Instead of begging him to take pity on us, we must think of something else; for if we do not succeed in tricking him, then we are lost. I have an idea – why don't you call up to him and ask him if he wants some wine?"

The Argonauts looked at one another in bewilderment, for there was not a drop of wine on board. But Jason realised the trick Medea had hidden up her sleeve and shouted out:

"Let us take on water, and you shall have the best wine in the world!" As soon as Talos heard the word 'wine', he let fall the stone he had lifted to throw on them, thus indicating that the strangers were free to row in close and leave the ship.

Meanwhile, Medea had taken a large cup and mixed Talos' 'wine', which was none other than water containing a strong perfume, and an even stronger sleeping-draught.

The heroes stepped ashore and saw the giant from close up. His look was savage, and his towering body the green of weathered bronze. It was madness to even think of fighting him, for with his heel alone he was capable of crushing two or three of the Argonauts to pulp. In spite of Talos' terrifying appearance, however, Medea walked boldly forward and handed him the cup. They all feared for her life, but Medea knew about this metal colossus and remained quite calm. Talos took the cup with a suspicious air. First he sniffed the drink, then rolled a little on his tongue; and while the Argonauts waited with bated breath for him to gulp it down, he looked them over slowly one by one, as if he had no intention of drinking. Not only that, but suddenly his look grew savage and he cried:

"Now there is no escape for you! I've led you to my very feet! One moment more, and then... "

They were all certain that moment was to be their last; but instead, Talos lifted high the cup and tossed the whole of Medea's potion down his throat in a single gulp. Then his features twisted into a smile of evil pleasure, and hurling the cup away he opened his great hands like talons, ready to fall upon the Argonauts like some huge bird of prey. But even as he did so, his knees began to buckle – Medea's magic brew had taken hold on him. He lurched towards the rocks to find support, but not even his hands could hold him upright any longer, and the bronze giant keeled over and lay full length upon the ground, covering a whole acre of fields with his huge body.

Medea looked at Talos' body with a searching eye and soon found his weak point.

... In spite of Talos' terrifying appearance, however, Medea walked boldly forward and handed him the cup...

"Take out that plug above his heel!" she shouted to Jason over the earth-shaking rumbles of the giant's snores.

Jason pulled out the plug, which stoppered one of Talos' veins like the bung in a barrel of wine; and as he did so, a fountain of colourless liquid shot skywards from the open vein. It was the giant's blood, draining from him in a torrent. Soon his snores grew weaker, and when the flow of liquid had died away to a trickle, so the last whisper of breath faded with it. Talos, the giant who never slept, would never wake again.

Freed now from his clutches, the Argonauts found the water they had come in search of. Then, since it was already late, they slept upon the shore and set off with the dawn.

All that day they voyaged smoothly on, but when night fell, they had a frightening experience. As they sailed by starlight, something very strange occurred. Little by little the stars began to lose their brightness, and in the end the darkness grew so murky that it presaged some terrible happening. Then the ship's lantern flickered and went out. They tried to relight it, but in vain. Not only could they not kindle a flame, but not a single spark rose from their flint, however hard they tried. None of the crew could imagine what fate now held in store for them. Since they could see nothing, did not know where they were going or what obstacle they might collide with, they let fall the oars. There was not a breath of wind, either, and nothing could be heard around the ship. They sat in black and deathly silence, totally ignorant of where they were or what awaited them.

Not even Lynceus, whose eyes could make out stars behind the clouds, could now distinguish anything. If he were only able to guess where the Pole Star lay, perhaps he would be able to guide them out of this accursed darkness. But in such conditions he could do nothing, and the icy fear of death sank its cold fingers deep into the hearts of all.

"Are we at sea still, or in Tartarus?" somebody whispered.

"Perhaps we are on the river Styx and being carried down to Hades" another voice muttered, while a third one added:

"The gods have never forgiven us. We cannot hope to see the light again. We shall live in inky darkness now for all eternity."

The Argonauts went on in this gloomy vein until it occurred to Jason that in this crisis the only one who could help them was Apollo, the god who drives the night before him.

"O great god of light!" he called. But before he could go on, his voice came echoing back out of the pitch-black depths: "O great god of light!"

"We are in the depths of Hades now for sure," the heroes thought – and sank into despair.

Yet Jason had not finished.

"O light-giver Apollo," he prayed, "son of Leto and mighty Zeus! Cast your rays into this fearsome night and bring the gift of hope to those who worship you!"

And while Jason's words still echoed and re-echoed, a sudden shaft of golden light scattered the deep gloom. They all gazed in wonder at the point from which it came, and saw on high, upon a towering black mass, the figure of Apollo streaming light and breaking up the darkness. The Argonauts now stared around them and saw that they were not beneath the arches of Hades, but between two mountainous rocks. Yet this by no means meant that they were on a safe course.

"These are the Black Rocks," warned Mopsus. "Whoever finds himself between them and does not know the exit goes straight on down to Hades."

"And who will lead us back onto our proper course?"

asked Idas.

"Apollo!" answered Jason, who had seen the god lift up his arm and show them the right way.

The Argonauts rushed to the oars and immediately began pulling in the direction the god had pointed. And indeed it was not long before they were out of that terrible dark passage and could clearly see the relief in one another's faces.

And now an island suddenly appeared before them, lit up by that same divine light. They rowed towards it, anxious to show their gratitude to the god who had rescued them. In a cave upon its shores they built a temple to him and called it the temple of Radiant Apollo, from the radiance in which the god had shown himself to them. Then they held athletic contests in his honour, while Orpheus played his lyre and sang hymns to the god. This festival founded by the Argonauts continued into early Christian times, and the island, whose name is Anaphe, was so called because it means in Greek that it suddenly appeared lit up, before the eyes of Jason and his companions.

The Black Rocks were the last peril the heroes faced on their voyage home. But a surprise of a different kind still lay in store for them upon their way. Euphemus suddenly remembered the ball of earth which had been given him by Triton. Taking it in his hands and looking at it curiously, he said to Jason:

"You are going home with the golden fleece to become king, while I am returning with a lump of clay – to become what?"

"Nobody knows if he is destined to become king or beggar, Euphemus," was Jason's answer. "Circe declared that the gods will never forgive me – to you a god has at least given a piece of earth."

"You speak as if I had been given a kingdom. It's a lump of earth Jason; and look what happens when you throw it." And with these words he tossed the lump into the sea.

But when it fell into the water, the earth did not dissolve or sink beneath the waves. Instead, before their astonished eyes, it began to swell and stretch until it was an islet. This islet went on growing until it was a large island. Then the island filled with greenery and flowers, trees and forests, fields of wheat and rolling vineyards. Next a fair city sprang up from the ground and filled with people. And last of all, these people, seeing the Argo, ran down to the shore crying:

"Our king has come! Welcome, Euphemus! Long live Euphemus our king!" And so, thanks to the ball of clay which Triton had presented to him, kind-hearted Euphemus, the fairest of the Argonauts, became the king of that new island, which today is known as Santorini.

As the Argo sailed away from its shores, Jason said to Medea:

"Euphemus has received his just reward. He was the most decent and fair-minded of us all. Will we, too, be rewarded for the suffering and ordeals we have gone through?"

"I do not think so, Jason," Medea replied. "The prize for the Argonauts' expedition has already been awarded – and Euphemus is the winner!"

"Is that the meaning of Euphemus' good fortune, then – or are you trying to say that we do not deserve the throne of Iolcus, even now when we have met the condition Pelias laid down?"

"What we deserve and what we get are very different things," Medea replied. "The throne of Iolcus is yours by right; but only pray that the gods do not pursue us further."

"Do you believe, then, they will go on hunting us?"

"I cannot rule it out, but they will no longer torture us upon the sea. The fact the prize has been awarded can only mean that the voyage of the Argonauts is drawing to its close."

Jason received no comfort from this answer. The fair omen of Euphemus' island, which meant they would reach Iolcus at last, was now completely overshadowed by the grim foreboding that the gods might not have wreaked full vengeance on them yet. But at least they had Hera on their side, and then Pelias had agreed that he would give up the throne if they returned bearing the golden fleece. That, for one, was sure.

Meanwhile, borne swiftly on the waves, the Argo had sailed into the gulf of Iolcus, and soon the buildings of the city came into sight.

When the heroes saw the city, their hearts leapt in their breasts. What dangers they had been through, and how many times they had looked death in the face! How long they had been separated from their homes and loved ones! But now they were returning in triumph, carrying the golden fleece which was destined to bring happiness to mankind. But would it? The heroes had their doubts. The gods who rule the world had pursued them without pity, and precisely when they had the precious talisman in their possession. What could that mean?

But this was no time for such gloomy thoughts. After all, they had carried off the most incredible feat the world had ever dreamed of, and brought their voyage to a successful conclusion even when the gods had placed well-nigh insuperable obstacles in their homeward path. Three years and three months had gone by since they set off. And now the great moment had come. With the golden fleece hung proudly on her mast, the Argo sailed into the harbour of Iolcus. A great crowd was gathered on the shore to greet them. Upright in the prow stood Jason, proudly pointing to the trophy of their incredible achievement. Too moved to speak, the Argonauts gazed at the assembled crowd. Orpheus plucked a few notes from his lyre, but he could not go on. Much as he wished to sing a glorious hymn of triumph, his voice broke in his throat, and his fingers trembled on the chords. Moist-eyed, the Argonauts brought their vessel to the quay and heaved the mooring-ropes across. And when, a moment later, the crew came streaming ashore, they fell into the open embrace of the people who were waiting for them.

The Argo had come home. The expedition of the Argonauts was finally concluded.

Unable to hold back his tears, Jason hugged his father and mother to his chest. How they had aged! What a dreadful trial it had been to his old parents, who had been coming daily to the shore for three years now in the hope that they would see the Argo sailing back over the horizon.

"But now it is all over," said Jason. "We have brought the golden fleece, and there will be happiness not for us alone, but everyone."

But, alas, it was not to be.

A DREAM UNREALISED

Pelias could not believe his eyes when he looked down from his palace and saw the Argo entering the harbour of Iolcus.

"And what is that gleaming in the sun upon her mast; surely it cannot be the golden fleece?" he asked himself uneasily. But it was – as a breathless soldier soon came running to inform him. Jason, whom he had sent to certain death, had not only returned but had brought the golden fleece as well. The impossible task had been carried out –

and the throne of Iolcus was the promised reward. Now what could Pelias do? It did not take the crafty king long to decide, and the next day, when Jason and nine of the Argonauts presented themselves at the palace, he was waiting for them with his answer.

"This valiant deed has won a kingdom for you!" he greeted Jason. "I have already begun to set my affairs in order, and in a few days I shall be ready to place the reins of power in your hands."

Although the Argonauts were surprised by Pelias' seeming willingness to hand his title over, not one of them suspected quite how false and hypocritical his offer was. For as soon as the last of Jason's comrades had left Iolcus, the king sent hired assassins to Aeson's house with orders to kill both him and his son. However, the killers were afraid to face the hero and lurked outside the house until they saw him leave.

When Jason returned, he was met by the sound of heart-rending sobs. Recognising his mother's voice, he pushed open the door to find her kneeling distraught over the lifeless body of his father. And worse was yet to come: fearing her son would fall a victim to Pelias' murdering frenzy too, she secretly took a rope and hanged herself to be spared the agony of a double loss.

Jason and Medea swore revenge. "Pelias must die," they vowed.

"And this can only be done with the aid of my magic arts," Medea added.

Next day, Medea went in search of Pelias' daughters.

"Jason and I wish to be reconciled with your father," she told them "and to show you how anxious we are to become your friends I can offer you a service no-one else on earth could render. I believe you know the power of my magic arts, and incredible though what I have to say may seem, it is the truth: I have the skill to make an old man young again. If you wish, I can restore your father to the bloom of youth."

"You sound sincere, yet we cannot possibly believe you," replied Pelias' daughters. "No-one has ever performed the miracle you speak of."

"Then bring me an old ram, and you shall see," replied Medea.

Consumed with curiosity, they went off and came back with a ram so old and feeble that it could scarcely stand.

"If I turn this doddering old creature into a young lamb," she challenged them, "will you believe that I can make your father young again?" And without listening to their exclamations of disbelief, Medea seized the ram by the horns and ordered:

"Bring me a knife and set a cauldron of water on the fire to boil!"

The daughters of Pelias looked at one another doubtfully, but hastened to carry out Medea's instructions. When all was ready, she slaughtered the beast, hacked it into pieces and dropped them in the cauldron to be boiled.

Pelias' daughters stared at her as if she were mad. Then, suddenly, the bubbling waters churned and a lively young lamb shot to the surface. It was incredible; the miracle had been performed. Medea was truly the greatest sorceress in the world. Shamed by their earlier disbelief, they begged her to forgive them and clamoured to know how their father could be made young again as well.

"It is very simple," Medea answered with a smile. "In the same way. And you do not even need my presence now. The spell is cast already, and your father will emerge from the cauldron as young and handsome as when he first became king of Iolcus."

Suspecting nothing, and fearlessly confident of the outcome, Pelias' daughters slipped into their father's room that night and killed him as he slept. Then, cutting up his body, they put the pieces in the pot to boil.

With bated breath, they waited for their father to spring

young and renewed from the seething waters – but in vain. The dark steam rose in clouds, but Pelias did not come to life again. Jason and Medea had taken a hideous revenge.

Yet Pelias' death did not help Jason to gain the kingdom of Iolcus. His son Acastus now ascended the throne. Though he had been an Argonaut, and one of Jason's closest friends, he was so angry when he learned the circumstances of his father's death that their friendship was wiped out and with it all memory of Pelias' murderous injustice. He took the crown as his by right, even though he had just given three years of his life to help Jason gain it. Now Jason and Medea were obliged to bid farewell to Iolcus and set sail in the Argo once again.

But first they had to make the journey to Orchomenus. When they arrived they climbed up Mount Laphystium, bearing the golden fleece, and dedicated it to Zeus. It was a moving scene. From this same spot the magic ram had once sailed off with Phrixus and Helle clinging to its neck; and now its golden pelt had been brought back. The promise was fulfilled – but there was no reward. The magic power of the fleece had faded, and all the hopes born with it had turned to idle dreams.

Jason and Medea climbed down Mount Laphystium to the sea and went on board the ship. They had decided to make their way southwards to Corinth. Both of them had links with this city, because it was now ruled by a relative of Jason's, the Aeolian Creon, a descendant of Sisyphus. Medea's father Aeëtes, too, had held the throne of Corinth before he moved to Colchis, for his father Helius was the divine protector of the city. And at Helius' command, Aeëtes had overseen the building of the temple to Aphrodite which stood high over the city on the rock of Acrocorinth.

When the Argo had brought them to the Isthmus, Jason and Medea beached her on the sand near the temple of Poseidon and walked on into Corinth.

Creon gave a warm greeting to the hero of the Argonauts' expedition and offered him and Medea a palatial house to live in. It seemed to the couple like a blessing from the gods after the cruel reception they had received at Iolcus.

In gratitude to Hera for all her help to Jason and his comrades, Medea built a temple to her on the slopes of Acrocorinth; and there, high on the mountainside, the sorceress who had served Hecate in her native land now gave thanks to Hera as a priestess in her shrine.

But this was in the early, happy days, when Jason and Medea were a truly loving couple. They lived a quiet life in

Corinth, and were blessed with four children whom they adored. Unfortunately, this love which had bloomed one perilous night in Colchis began in time to fade and slowly wither, until at last disaster struck.

THE TRAGIC END

At first their happiness was only marred by minor quarrels which neither of them gave much importance to. Little by little, however, more serious causes were added to the list. Medea began to feel ill at ease in her new homeland. However hard she tried, she could not win the affection of the Corinthians, who regarded her as a foreigner and, what was worse, a witch. There were even some among them who seized the opportunity provided by every misfortune or natural disaster to whisper: "It's all the witch's fault; before she came we never had such storms and droughts!" As time went by, more and more of the city's people began to hate Medea – and even those who did not believe she brought ill-luck upon them were not disposed to treat her as a friend. They all forgot how much she had helped Jason and the other Argonauts. It was enough for them that she had magic powers, which they regarded as an evil to be feared. There were no witches in Greece; such creatures and their sorcery belonged only in distant and barbaric lands. Whenever they spoke of Medea, they avoided her name, calling her only 'that foreign sorceress'. They even regarded her children with suspicion and would not let their own youngsters play with them. Swayed by his people's hostility, Creon, too, avoided her and began inviting Jason to the palace without his wife.

It was Medea who bore the brunt of this unfriendly atmosphere, while Jason thoughtlessly continued his visits to the royal household where he spent pleasant hours in Creon's company.

Ten years had now gone by since the couple first came to Corinth, and Medea was growing ever more unhappy. Irritated by the miserable atmosphere in his own house, Jason reacted by spending even more of his time with Creon, often staying all night at the palace. And when he did go home, he would feel worse still – for added to her own and her children's isolation Medea now knew the bitterness of her husband's absence, and was not slow to voice her anger. Returning from a night at Creon's, Jason would often find his wife in tears; but instead of trying to put himself in her position he simply grew colder and more distant. And when he was at home, the pair of them did nothing but quarrel like the worst of enemies. Indeed, had it not been for the children, Jason might have left home altogether. Thus the love which had flared up so brightly in distant Colchis, now slowly burned to ashes. A tragedy was about to unfold.

Creon had a daughter, Glauce, who was both young and beautiful; and the more Jason was repelled by Medea's endless complaints, the more he was drawn to this girl's company.

One evening, Creon said to him:

"I notice, my friend, that you are no longer happy with your wife – and I cannot say I blame you. How can you love a creature that everybody hates – especially when I see you have taken a liking to Glauce? Listen Jason, I have no son to hand my kingdom down to when I die, so I propose you take my daughter's hand in marriage. If you agree, I will give you half my kingdom now, and the remainder shall be yours when I am gone. You did not become a king in Iolcus, but you will be one in Corinth. Besides, this marriage will be not only for your own good, but for mine, my daughter's and for all of Corinth. Flattering courtiers hover round Glauce like flies around a honeypot, counting the days until I die so they can seize my throne. Glauce despises them as much as I do, and will be miserable all her days if one of them succeeds in marrying her. Take her for yourself, and the ladder to the throne will be pulled from beneath their feet. I know you will not deny me this, but I cannot wait to hear you say so."

All Jason did was lower his head. While Creon waited for the answer, he sat dumb.

"Aren't you pleased by my suggestion?" Creon asked him.

Jason said nothing. He was engulfed by memories.

He thought back to that time beneath the moon when he had found Medea and been given hope. He thought of how he had obtained the strength to yoke the bulls and defeat the giant warriors in Ares' field; of how he had been enabled to foil the dragon and snatch the golden fleece. Then he thought of Apsyrtus, whose own sister had let him go to his death so that the Argonauts might be saved. He remembered the fearful ordeals they had been put through by the wrathful gods, and their agonies of weary thirst in the desert, when he had reached the decision to die in Medea's arms beneath the blazing sun. "I am despicable," he told himself.

"Why do you not answer, Jason?" Creon enquired. "I'd expected my proposal to delight you."

Jason got to his feet.

"My thanks to you, Creon," he replied, "but I cannot do it." And without another word he left the palace and made straight for home.

Medea had not set eyes on him for days – and when she did so, she erupted. The quarrel that broke out that evening was like a raging storm.

The very next morning, Jason went back to the palace and told Creon:

"I accept your offer."

Many more days had now gone by, and Jason had still not returned home. One morning, Medea noticed an unusual bustle in the city. Since nobody would speak to her, she could not learn why all the citizens were thronging the streets dressed in their finest robes.

"Some festival is going on that I had no idea of," she told herself. "I shall go to the market-place to see what is happening."

When she reached the main street of the city she saw a wedding procession approaching, with gilded chariots and banners.

"Is the king marrying, then?" Medea wondered. "It could be that – why, anything is possible these days." She wanted to ask one of the bystanders, but they all looked at her strangely and edged away. "What hatred!" she muttered. "Ye gods, what have I done to them?" She half made up her mind to leave, but curiosity held her there. "Perhaps

Creon is marrying off his daughter," she told herself at last. "Yes, that is it. I must stay to see whom she has taken and learn who Corinth's next king will be." With this in mind, she found an inconspicuous vantage-point and waited for the wedding procession to draw near.

Of course, the figures standing in the gilded chariot were none other than Jason and Glauce. Behind the couple followed Creon and after him a string of chariots bearing the kings of other cities, all invited to the marriage of the lovely princess with the leader of the Argonauts. Radiant with happiness, Glauce clung to Jason's arm, while Jason himself smiled to think that the gods had remembered him at last. "The hour of my reward has come," he told himself, "and perhaps the throne of Corinth is worth even more than that of Iolcus." But his happy thoughts were interrupted by a shriek of rage. Medea, like a thing possessed, had burst out from the crowd and hurled herself upon the chariot. In a frenzy of anger she struck Jason repeated blows in the face, sank her nails deep into his cheeks and kicked wildly at him, all the while screaming out:

"There, you traitor! Take that, you ungrateful wretch! Where are your vows of everlasting fidelity, you monster? Have you forgotten your honour and your duty to the woman who gave up all the world for you? You'll live to

... "And you, too, will pay!" she shrieked, stabbing a trembling finger at Glauce...

curse the day you broke your faith with me! Now you will pay for all the neglect and humiliation I have suffered at your hands! And you, too, will pay!" she shrieked, stabbing a trembling finger at Glauce. "And you Creon, and all of you." And her vengeful hand swept over the horrified crowd. "Now you will see the Medea you have spurned! You think you hated me? Now you will see what hatred means – the hatred that you planted, fed and watered in my heart, you fools, till now it bursts in ripeness on you all, like a curse sent by the gods!"

That was all Medea had the time to say – but yet it was enough. Creon's guards pulled her from the chariot, and with kicks, blows and curses she was dragged away from the procession. Though Medea's wild assault may have robbed the ceremony of its dignity, it did not prevent the wedding going forward. The marriage of Jason and Glauce took place as arranged – but whatever dreams that couple now had for the future, Medea's plans were very different. The moment she found herself alone, she sat down and began to scheme revenge.

Her golden eyes glowed savagely as she wove a devilish plot to bring ruin and destruction upon the guilty and the innocent alike. So murderous was her hatred that she cared not if the two-edged blade of vengeance wounded her as well. But suddenly her train of thought was interrupted. Her door flew open and Creon himself burst furiously into her room.

"Vile sorceress!" he cried. "You betrayed your father and your country, you killed your own brother for the sake of your sick lusts. I know your power, but don't imagine I will let you harm us. You and your vile brats will leave Corinth immediately. Get ready at once. I have given orders to my men to take you off to foreign parts and I want no objections. My decision is final!" With these words he turned on his heel and strode out.

The edict struck Medea like a thunderbolt. "I shall never rest till I have wreaked revenge," she said. "All I need is a little time. One day will be sufficient to spread ruin. I mustn't let them drag me off immediately."

Moments later, Jason arrived. He burst in like a furious storm, ready to hurl himself on her and wring her neck.

Medea froze. At this critical point she must not let her anger show itself again. Putting on a show of remorse so masterly that Jason did not even begin to suspect that it was feigned, she began to confess:

"I am guilty! I deserve the harshest punishment you can devise. Whip me, curse me, kill me if you will. I deserve it all!"

Medea's act had the desired effect. Jason softened towards her.

"Why did you do such a thing?" he asked.

"I was to blame, I know," Medea sobbed, "but now the time has come to pay. Creon has banished us from Corinth. For me, that is a just punishment. I deserve to be reduced to beggary and die of hunger and neglect. But, alas, he has ordered our children to be banished, too!"

"Our children as well?" gasped Jason.

"Yes. What will become of them? Who will take care of them in foreign lands? If I die, it is no more than I deserve, but what have the children done to merit such a fate? Jason, you must help me save them."

"For their sake, I will do anything you wish," the hero promised.

"Traitor!" Medea muttered to herself. "Now you fall headlong into the trap I have laid for you!" But aloud she said:

"This is what you must do. Go to the palace and say what you have seen. Tell Creon: 'Medea is truly repentant, understands her fault, and wishes to leave Corinth of her own accord in order to forget. But she needs a day to make her preparations; after all, she has been living ten years in this city.' Add, too, that to make up for the harm that I have done to Glauce I am preparing gifts for her that I will send tomorrow: a splendid robe and a wreath of solid gold to place upon her brows. I will send the children with these presents, to beg Glauce to intercede on their behalf and persuade king Creon not to banish them from Corinth."

"I am glad to see you are ready to undo the trouble you have caused" said Jason. "Everything will be done as you have planned."

"I hope so!" Medea replied – but Jason did not notice the cruel satisfaction that glinted in her eyes as she spoke the words.

The unsuspecting Creon finally agreed to let her stay just one more day, and this gave Medea all the time she needed to work her magic on the gown and diadem she had promised Glauce. On one side they shone fair and beautifully worked, but on the other they were steeped in a deadly poison that only Medea had the skill to brew.

Next morning, when her work was finished and the robe and diadem neatly laid out in a box, Medea called her two eldest children to her and gave instructions to take the gifts to Glauce and beg her to persuade her father to let her four children remain in Corinth.

Glauce was reluctant to accept the presents, but on seeing the magnificent robe she would now appear in at great festivals, and the gleaming beauty of the diadem which would adorn her brow, she was overcome with joy and willingly agreed to speak to her father.

When the youngsters returned, Medea looked at them with questioning anxiety. "Will my magic work on her?" she wondered. "Will Glauce wear my gifts or not?" But when she learned that the mere sight of them had been enough to send the princess into transports of delight, a savage joy welled up inside her. "Yes, my plan will succeed," she told herself.

She did not have long to wait. Soon afterwards, a servant of the king burst wildly into the house.

"Get out of our city, evil sorceress!" he cried. "Disaster has fallen upon Corinth, and you are the cause!"

"Come in and tell me everything," said Medea with a welcoming gesture. "You bring me pleasant news!"

"I bring the vilest news that tongue can tell, and I would choke the life out of you if I did not fear to touch a sorceress. Hear the whole story, though, and learn the hideousness of your crime. Glauce put on the robe that you had sent her and stood before her mirror lost in admiration, for it made her look ten times more beautiful than ever. Suspecting nothing, she then laid the golden wreath upon her brows. 'What a splendid diadem!' she murmured. Then suddenly she let out a cry of terror. 'Help! I am burning!' she screamed. The robe you had given her was clinging to her body and had begun to boil and give off clouds of smoke. The diadem scorched her forehead like a red-hot iron. Her father came running at her cries. 'Father, the witch's cursed gifts are burning me!' she wailed. 'Save me if there is still time!' Her wretched father tried to pull the robe away, from her body, but it not only clung to her the tighter but burst into flame. Creon tried again, though he could see the fire threatened him as well, but the material stuck to his arms and legs and the flames flared up and embraced them both. Locked together like blazing torches, father and daughter ran screaming through the palace, while everything they touched burst into flames. Soldiers and servants came running to answer their despairing cries; but they too were swallowed by the hungry yellow tongues. The whole palace was set ablaze. Glauce, Creon and all who tried to help died in the fire. Now there is nothing but a heap of ashes there, and all Corinth mourns the worst calamity that has ever befallen the city. How I escaped I do not know. Some god must have saved me."

"And Jason?" Medea demanded. "What happened to that traitor?"

"No, witch, you will not have that pleasure! Jason escaped unharmed."

"So much the worse for him. I have a harsher punishment in store!"

"Sorceress! Murderer! Leave Corinth before we tear you into pieces!"

"Not until I have crushed him utterly; not till I have revenged myself on him by the vilest crime a mother could devise!"

The servant's hair stood on end when he heard these words.

"She is a tigress, not a woman!" he cried, and fled in terror of her. Medea was left standing there alone.

"Now the last, most dreadful act of the whole drama remains to be played out. Now he will learn the meaning of ingratitude! Now he will see what treachery means! And all the world will soon recoil before the horror that is called Medea! But I must hesitate no longer. The more this hurts me, the sharper his own suffering will be. What if I pay for his grief in the dearest coin of all? That is the price must be exacted for a punishment to fit a traitor such as he!"

And moments later the fearsome sorceress had committed the most hideous deed of all, the crime no mother's hands are capable of.

Hardly was it completed when Jason appeared in the

doorway. Little suspecting what new blow awaited him, he came into her room. Shattered with grief, he did not shout, but simply said:

"Have you had your fill of vengeance now?"

"My hunger will be satisfied soon enough, when I see you writhe in misery. Open that door!"

Jason looked at her in bewilderment. What did she mean? Why should he open the door? To see what?

"Open that door and see what the vengeance of Medea means!"

Hesitantly, Jason pushed the door aside.

Horror of horrors! At his feet lay the dead bodies of two of his children! "O gods!" he cried. "Why have you punished me so harshly? Was I so much to blame? Yet I have been deeply at fault: first when I lured Apsyrtus to his death, and now for breaking the vow I gave in the face of deadly peril. I am an ungrateful traitor and can hold no god to account for my misfortunes. I alone am guilty!"

He came out of the children's room a broken man. With his head sunk on his chest he stood before Medea. He could have killed her if he wished, but there was no fight left in him, Besides, what was there to gain by slaughtering her now?

"How could you do it?" was all that he could say, and

burying his face in his hands he burst into bitter sobs of grief.

Jason stumbled out onto the road weeping inconsolably at the loss of his dear children, while Medea watched him go with a look of satisfaction blended with undying hatred. But when at last he had dragged himself out of sight she went back to the children's room, threw herself upon the innocent dead creatures and sobbed her heart out in her turn. For with her own hands she had slain the children whom she loved so much. This was how the gods had punished her for everything at last – for rejecting her father and her country and for betraying her own brother to satisfy her lust.

Medea lay there weeping for long hours, but at last she rose and wiped away her tears. Then she brought water, washed her children's bodies and having dressed them in their funeral robes she carried them up to Acrocorinth and buried them by that same temple of Hera which she herself had built.

Of course, Medea could no longer stay in Corinth. Her grandfather Helius, the only god who felt any sympathy for her, realised this and sent a chariot drawn by winged dragons to aid her escape. Upon it Medea placed the two children who had not fallen to her murdering fury and then flew far away.

Not long afterwards she married Aegeus, king of Athens. Her dearest wish was to make one of her own sons his successor, but Theseus stood in her way and so she was at last obliged to flee to her own country. There she found that her father had meanwhile been deposed. But with her magic powers she helped him to regain the throne and was at last reconciled with him. Later her son Medus became king of the neighbouring country which was known as Media ever afterwards.

It is said that Medea never died, that so great were her magic powers that even Death went in fear of her. And so the most terrible sorceress the world had ever known lived on to offer her protection to all witches, those creatures who so rarely work for good but more often spread ruin and grief wherever they cast their spells.

Perhaps some god had forgiven Medea for her hideous crime, but mortals never did. Ever since, the word Medea has meant 'murderess', and indeed the murderess who commits the most horrible crime a woman is capable of.

And Jason?

As for Jason, that once mighty hero now sought some crumb of consolation for his loss, but found it nowhere. All sense of purpose gone, he wandered helplessly from place to place. Time heals all wounds, men say, but for Jason's grief there was no cure. The fearless Argonaut had been abandoned by both men and gods.

For years he drifted aimlessly; like a dry leaf carried on the wind, until at last he found himself once more at the temple of Poseidon, on the Isthmus of Corinth.

"Somewhere hereabouts we once left the Argo on the sands," Jason remembered, and his blood began to pulse with memories of past adventures. "What can have become of her? Where is she now?" As he spoke, his eye fell on the ruin of a ship. "Surely it cannot be that old, battered hulk?" he wondered, swallowing back the tears as he approached it.

It was indeed the Argo, worm-eaten and consumed by time. The head of Hera still stood at her helm, but wind and sun had done their work here, too, and the cracked and storm-scoured figurehead was no longer recognisable.

Who was left to shield Jason now and lend him aid? No-one, not even the goddess Hera, who had always held him under her protection.

How much had happened since those distant days! But now the glory had all faded. How fair the Argo had been once – and what was she now? How proudly Hera's head had once gazed forward from the prow – and now what was left of her? How brilliant were the achievements of your youth, Jason – and what have you sunk to now? Where are the wealth and happiness the golden fleece once seemed to promise? What power, indeed, controls the destiny of men?

His mind confused and wearied by these questions, Jason stretched out in the shade cast by the Argo's bows, and there sleep overtook him. He never opened his eyes again – for while he slept a strong wind blew up, the rotten timbers of the Argo swayed and creaked, and Hera's heavy figurehead came crashing down on Jason and crushed the life from him.

Thus died the man who had escaped a thousand dangers. The goddess Hera, who had been his constant guardian, had killed her favourite at last. Did she mean to kill him? Was it a punishment? No one ever learned.

The leader of the Argonauts was dead, but by their deeds he and his comrades had won eternal glory. The proof of this can be seen not only in the millions of people all over the world who have read and admired the countless retellings of their voyage, but in the lively interest of the many researchers who have tried to establish either the exact route followed by these bold seafarers or the real reasons which sent them out upon their great adventure. A number of them now claim that the golden fleece, that jealously-guarded charm which brought wealth and plenty to its possessors, was none other than gold, the precious metal which wields such power in the world. Yet whether the Argonauts returned loaded with gold or not, their great achievement stands. By their daring and determination they opened new routes across uncharted seas, seas which men's fears and fantasies had filled with hideous monsters and deadly perils. Thanks to the boldness of these heroes the Symplegades rocks would never again bar the way to mariners, and within a few centuries Greek ships were to plough the seas from Colchis on the shores of the Black Sea to the coasts of France and Spain, setting up new cities and bringing civilisation to both East and West.

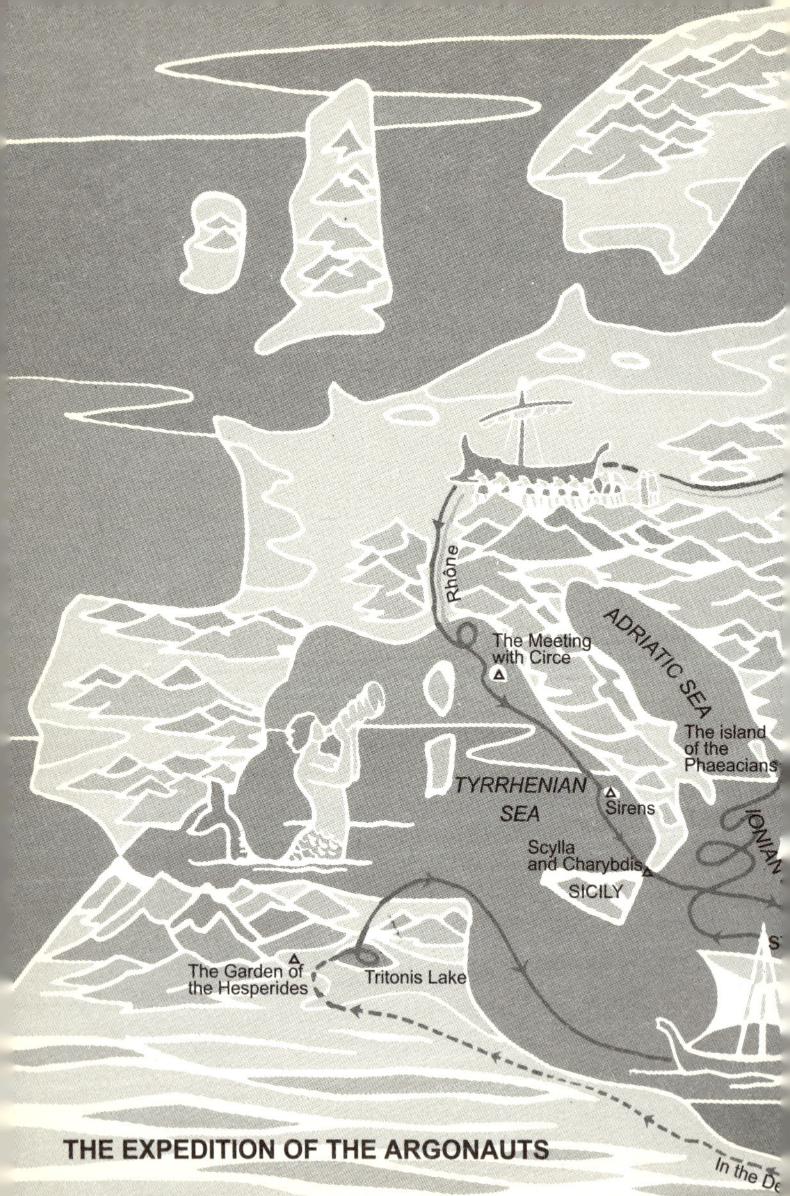

THE EXPEDITION OF THE ARGONAUTS

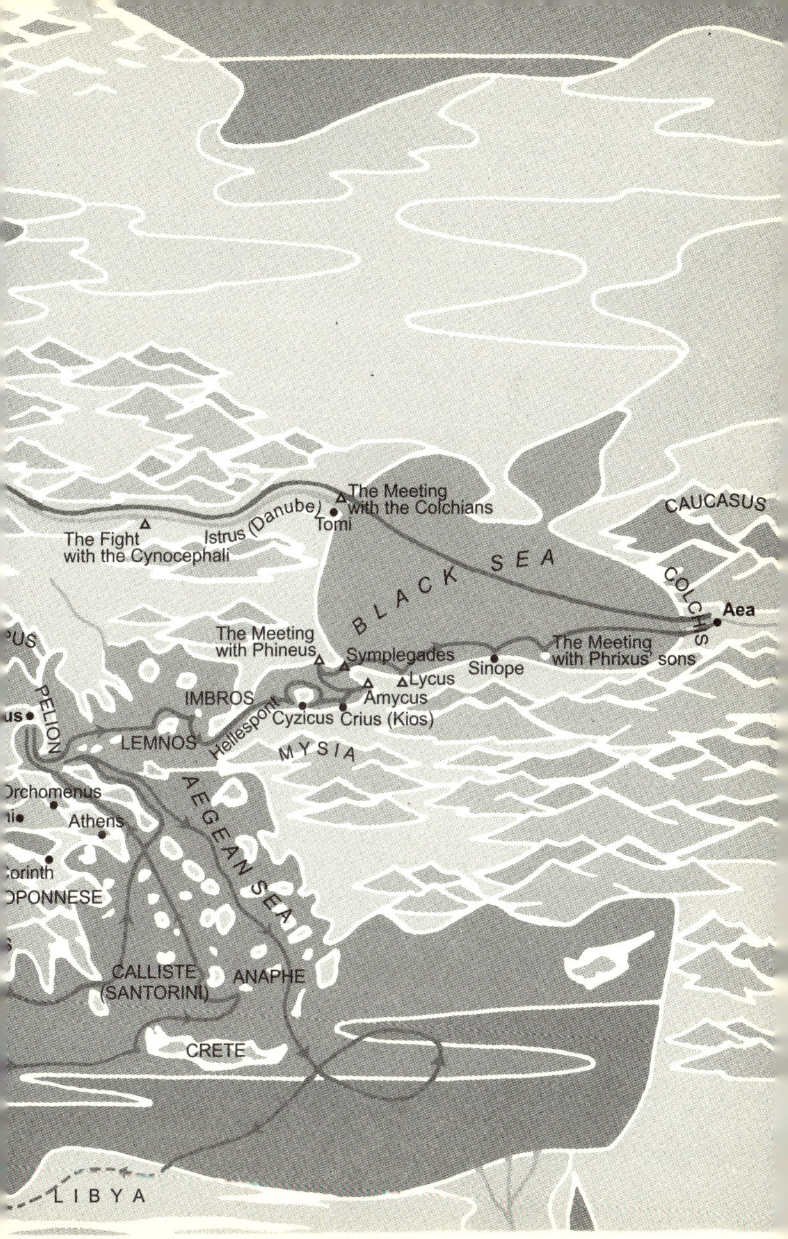
The Meeting with the Colchians
Tomi
Istrus (Danube)
The Fight with the Cynocephali
CAUCASUS
BLACK SEA
COLCHIS
Aea
The Meeting with Phineus
Symplegades
Sinope
The Meeting with Phrixus' sons
Lycus
Amycus
IMBROS
Cyzicus
Crius (Kios)
Hellespont
LEMNOS
MYSIA
PELION
AEGEAN SEA
Athens
CALLISTE (SANTORINI)
ANAPHE
CRETE
LIBYA